PSYCHOLOGICAL S

W9-CJZ-547

# Going Nowhere

### A NOVEL BY

## Alvin Greenberg

SIMON AND SCHUSTER
New York

PS
3557
R377
G6

All rights reserved
including the right of reproduction
in whole or in part in any form
Copyright © 1971 by Alvin Greenberg
Published by Simon and Schuster
Rockefeller Center, 630 Fifth Avenue
New York, New York 10020

FIRST PRINTING

SBN 671–20957–4
Library of Congress Catalog Card Number: 71–154102
Designed by Irving Perkins
Manufactured in the United States of America
By H. Wolff Book Mfg. Co., Inc., New York, N.Y.

This book is dedicated
to all the members
of the Poughkeepsie Institute,
wherever they are.

# Contents

PART I

# The Beginning

# Chapter 1

ONCE UPON a time a young assistant professor of physics with a Ph.D. from a highly rated Eastern institution and a tenured associate professorship in the immediate offing had a violent asthma attack in the second-floor men's room of the large Midwestern state university where he taught a little and researched mostly but on this occasion was so wracked by a series of coughs and spasms that he fell against a wash-basin, jarring loose his glasses, which tumbled to the tile floor and shattered, both lenses, so that when this young professor's most promising senior student, who already had in his clutches a prestigious and high-paying fellowship to his mentor's alma mater, came strolling into the men's room without any shoes on, for it was both a season and an era when undergraduates, even in the physical sciences, preferred to go barefoot, the first thing he did, seeing his professor kneeling and sobbing against the washstand, and rushing to his side to aid him, was to step down firmly upon a mass of splinters of glass from the broken lenses, a good many of which lodged themselves painfully into the sole of his foot and not all of which were removed later that afternoon, by the medical student who worked as an assistant at the student health service, with the result that those splinters that had become hidden deep in the flesh soon produced a severe infection there, that led first to pain, and then to swelling, and at last, in due time, having been ignored long enough while this young physics major completed his brilliant senior honors thesis, to the amputation of the left leg just below the knee three days before graduation and three months and three days before the young man left for graduate school, as brilliant as ever before but extremely disconsolate, so that though his scholarly performance was unexcelled it was not many months before he addressed to his father a brief, formal note simply requesting that his name be removed from his father's will and left the study of theoretical physics for ever and ever, as his young mentor, who now lived in a small town in the Southwest, whither all serious asthmatics bend, where he tooled leather, experimented with pots and glazes, and lived comfortably off the not insubstantial income from investments his scientific insights had led him to while still a graduate student himself, had already done.

In good time it could have been expected that the one-legged ex-student might, in his wanderings, have hobbled into the town where the asthmatic ex-professor dwelt and that there the two might have spotted each other, outside the town's only café, and stepped inside, to rejoice with, or console, one another, over strong drink, or, on the other hand, there the two might never have met, the ex-professor stepping unknowingly inside the bar just seconds before the ex-student, thirsty but indigent, passed in front of the bar, looking longingly but hopelessly at its silent exterior, and proceeded on out the far end of the town, not many yards beyond.

Nothing of the kind happened, however. The ex-student preferred to confine his wanderings to the East Coast. In the spring he hitchhiked northward, through Georgia and the Carolinas, Virginia, the District of Columbia, where he always made a point of pausing briefly, then on to Maryland and Delaware and Pennsylvania and New Jersey, across New York and Connecticut and on upward into New England, ending up on the Maine coast as summer began and there attaching himself to some fashionable resort, where for the rest of the summer he could manage a living by washing the dusty cars of vacationers. Then as the vacationers departed and the fall closed in, he would make his way back toward the South, down through New England and across the Middle Atlantic states and down along the Southeastern coast, always staying as close to the shoreline as was compatible with the best highways and the most traffic, until at last he came to a rest in some pleasant seaside city in Florida, where, at a fashionable resort, he could spend the winter washing the dusty cars of vacationers. His sad physical plight was a boon for hitchhiking. He was rarely at the roadside long enough to lift his thumb before a kindly motorist stopped for him. And if there was often considerable embarrassment over the problem of where to stow his crutches when he entered these vehicles, he soon brought an end to any discomfort as they traveled on, regaling his hosts with stories of how he had lost his leg hunting alligators in Florida, or bears in Maine, of how he was traveling north to rejoin his twin sister, whom he had never seen since the two of them had been cast into separate orphanages at a very early age, or south to reclaim the paternal lands at Boca Raton which his wily uncle, the executor of the family estate, had mortgaged away to pay for his own gambling debts.

All of these stories were highly entertaining and had three things in common: each included a sister, a germ of truth, and a high moral goal, at the achievement of which all would once again be right with the world. He had, for example, once paddled a canoe from which a would-be poacher had taken several futile shots at alligators in the Everglades before leaping up in anger and dumping both of them into the swamp. At a Maine hotel one summer he had spent a good many mornings cleaning up the mess that bears had made by dumping over garbage cans in the night. There was, in his past, either a true paternal estate or a truly Dostoievskian uncle, he could no longer remember which. Once, on his first journey up the coast, when he was not yet used to maneuvering along the roadside on crutches and had to take long rests, he had spent an entire day sitting on the grass in front of an orphanage near Baltimore, watching cars go in and out on the gravel drive. On a moonlit highway in North Carolina he had watched a truck crash through the guardrail of a bridge and scatter its load of gleaming white hogs across the surface of the dark water below. He had been leaning against the iron bars of the fence on Pennsylvania Avenue one spring morning when a young woman in the line of tourists waiting to enter the White House had taken a heavy automatic out of her purse and rammed a loaded clip into its handle and then put it away again and closed up her purse, and moved on ahead with the line. And a year later he had been sleeping in the bushes beside a bridge on the Connecticut Turnpike, out of choice rather than necessity, because he was comforted by the landscaping of that particular highway, when, shortly before dawn, a flying saucer had landed within a dozen yards of him, and a door in its side had slid silently open, and his own name had been called out. But he never told any stories about that, because when that happened, his hitch-hiking days were over, at least as he had known them.

So much for the germ of truth. As for the sister, he had never had one, so far as he knew, or a brother either, but it took only a few years of journeying up and down the coast before her constant appearances in his stories began to endow her with a certain reality, and he began to wonder whether he had not, indeed, had a real sister after all, who had at some time been secreted away from him, like the fate of the hog-truck driver, or the President, or his paternal estate. One way or another, he simply enjoyed her presence in his stories, though the idea of having a sister had never occurred to him prior to the beginning of his travels. He was also aware of how things changed, when she entered the story, between the teller and his audience. For it was always in her service that he had tangled with wild beasts, plunged into icy rivers, fought the inhumanity and injustice of the courts, and, indeed, committed himself to the painful journey he was now embarked upon. Each time he told a story he changed her name, or her appearance, or both.

The high moral goals were sufficient, each, unto the stories thereof: rescue of the sister, the land, the President, or the humble laborers who kept the wheels of the nation turning—how could all fail to go right after such deeds as those?

# Chapter 2

H O W  A L L  C O U L D, indeed, fail to go right after such deeds as those was precisely what he found out after—but not, of course, immediately after—he entered the flying saucer that landed beside him where he lay peacefully sleeping in the bushes beside a bridge on the Connecticut Turnpike just before the dawn of a lovely day in late spring. The bridge was fieldstone, the bushes were lilac, just on the verge of blooming, the highway was practically deserted, and the saucer, which was not overlarge, lay throbbing quietly in the dark for a while, as if catching its breath, before at last a door in its side slid silently open, and the beam of light that poured through it splashed brightly among the lilacs, and a voice from its interior began to call softly, "Arthur, Arthur."

Arthur, sound asleep, had been dreaming of rescuing his sister, a slender, long-legged blonde, almost a child still, from the clutches of an enormous octopus that had come swarming ashore as the two of them picnicked one evening on the beach at Sandy Point, Cape Cod, and had swept her up, flaxen hair gleaming in the dying rays of the sun, with one of its thick slimy tentacles while fending him off and tangling him up in several others, so that when the sudden burst of yellow light fell upon him it was as if someone had suddenly relit the abandoned lighthouse that still stood on the point there, and with such a brilliance that the monster dropped his prey and shriveled up and fled back into the sea, whence he had come, while Arthur sat up, dazed, still feeling the enormous pressure of the suction cups on his nonexistent leg, trying to disentangle his remaining leg from the thick roots of a lilac bush, and suddenly aware that he knew the voice that was calling to him from behind all that light. It was the voice of his former mentor, Professor Melville.

"Coming!" cried Arthur, scrambling to his foot, though he was completely baffled by the alacrity of his response to a voice he had not thought of for many years and that represented a period of his life that he had no desire at all to be reminded of. Neither, for that matter, did he have any reason to believe that it really was the voice of Professor Melville, calling to him in such a place, and from such a source. Nonetheless, he hobbled hastily forward on his shabby wooden crutches, his body twisted to one side in order to balance the knapsack he had flung over his shoulder by one strap only. As he approached the saucer, a small ramp slid forward from the base of the doorway, hovered tentatively in mid-air, and then settled gently to the ground in his path. When he stepped upon it, it rose from the ground and withdrew slowly into the saucer, like a slender metallic tongue, taking him with it, until he was inside, and the door slid shut noiselessly behind him.

Much to his surprise there was no one in the saucer, neither Professor Melville nor the crew that, now that he began to give some thought to what was happening to him, he had expected to find there. The saucer consisted of a single room, rather larger than he had anticipated, tastefully decorated in golds and browns, and filled with the warm yellow glow of its indirect lighting. Around its circumference were a dozen comfortable-looking armchairs, all facing toward the center, and it was to one of these that Arthur went when a different voice from the one which had called to him spoke out and ordered him to take a seat and fasten his safety belt. When he had dumped his knapsack into the neighboring seat and laid his crutches on the floor beside his own chair and strapped himself in, he was about to speak up for the first time, and ask the whereabouts of Professor Melville, when the voice that had ordered him to his seat came on again.

"Professor Melville," it said, "is not here at this time. We shall rendezvous with him shortly. Please remain seated at all times during take-off and flight. This ship is operating under its automatic control and guidance system. As the voice of that system, I request your complete cooperation at all times."

The voice repeated "times" three times and then shut off. The yellow light dimmed and a ring of bluish light lit up around the ceiling. A deep buzz and a heavy vibration came from beneath his feet, and Arthur gripped the arms of his chair. The yellow light went out completely. The buzz and vibration toned down to a more solemn level. At last, as Arthur was in the midst of tightening his seat belt one more time, he felt the saucer begin to move. But instead of the smooth burst of power and the freedom of flight he had expected, it seemed to be struggling to rise, lurched toward one side, and then settled back down again. The engines began to vibrate heavily once more. The blue light around the ceiling flickered, blinked out, came back on again, and held steady. Arthur clung tightly to the arm rests. The whole saucer vibrated. Then, quite suddenly, the engines shut off and all fell silent and motionless.

After sitting for a long time in the silence and semidarkness, with the halo of bluish light glowing above him, Arthur gradually relaxed his grip on the arm rests and loosened his seat belt. And as more time passed, and neither the voice nor the engines showed any further signs of activity, he unfastened his seat belt altogether and stood up, holding to the side of the chair until he had got his crutches under his arms, and then began to look around him. Just behind his chair, as behind each chair, he found that there was a small round depression in the wall, and by pressing a button on its edge he was able to cause the metal disc which covered it to slide aside and reveal the window inset there. When he pressed his nose to the pane, he had no trouble at all in seeing where they were.

They were next to the bridge, in the midst of the lilac bushes where he had been sleeping. Arthur remembered it was Memorial Day. The sky was beginning to turn gray with dawn and he could see that the traffic had begun to pick up on the Turnpike, most of it in the southbound lane, on the other side of the highway. What were the chances, he wondered, of some holiday traveler spotting the saucer where it lay among the bushes, and thinking it to be something besides a piece of highway maintenance equipment? He hobbled over to the doorway, hardly expecting that it would open at his mere presence. It didn't. He returned to the window. The sky was rapidly growing lighter. The cars that were going by no longer had their headlights on. The first flickers of sunlight caught in the bushes. He watched as a sprig of lilac, just inches beyond the window, opened into bloom. As a brilliant undergraduate, he had never quite known what to make of flying-saucer phenomena and had often found himself arguing both sides of the question. He had no trouble at all making a convincing statistical case for the probability of other sentient beings in the universe of a higher order of intelligence than man. He also had sufficient knowledge to demonstrate with equal ease the unlikelihood of any possibility for intergalactic transport. He no longer recalled either the scientific facts on which he had based those arguments or the rhetorical subtleties by means of which he had proved them both true. Even now he didn't know just where he stood on the flying-saucer question. He wished someone would speak up and clarify it for him. Just then the yellow light burst on again in full force, the saucer shuddered and gave a mighty jerk, so that Arthur's crutches slipped out from under him and he was tossed backward, banging his head soundly against the metal back of the chair and dropping unconscious to the floor as the saucer spun about for a moment just above the bushes, gleaming brightly in the early-morning sunlight, and then angled upward, sliced into a corner of the bridge, showering the roadside with fieldstone chips, wobbled out into the air over the highway, regained its balance, and sped away into the pale blue spring sky.

# Chapter 3

W HEN ARTHUR awoke from a dream in which his sister had led him unerringly out of a complex subterranean labyrinth after he had done battle in its central chamber with an enormous red bull painted with the signs of the zodiac, his absent leg throbbed from the goring he had received, his hands ached from the pressure with which he had at last gripped the monster's horns and twisted and twisted till the thick neck snapped and the great beast slumped to the ground at his feet, and the engines of the saucer hummed softly and reassuringly beneath him. Only the dullest glow of the yellow light filled the room as he pulled his crutches to him, raised himself from the floor, and turned toward the small round window again. The metal cover was closed once more—no doubt, thought Arthur, as a protection against the hazards of extreme acceleration—but he knew where the button was now and quickly opened it, expecting to find out there only the dark, star-flecked depths of space.

What he saw, instead, was a bleak, flat, dismal, empty landscape the likes of which he had never seen before. The saucer appeared to be hovering just a few feet above a brackish, lifeless swamp. A thick, green, deadly-looking liquid spread out below and around it, gaseous bubbles occasionally bursting thickly through its surface. A gray and seemingly unbreathable miasma hung motionless over the surface. Farther on, the swamp was filled with clumps of dead, spiky weeds, and beyond them, far out on the horizon, clustered ugly yellow clouds, streaked with black. A more inhospitable place for life Arthur thought he had never seen.

"My god," he muttered, backing away from the window and toward the center of the room, "where could this be?" The yellow lights slowly brightened and revealed a figure seated in a chair on the opposite side of the room which answered his question.

"New Jersey," it said, softly.

"Professor Melville," cried Arthur, hobbling rapidly forward on his crutches. "Sir!" He stopped, confounded, in the center of the saucer's large cabin. The lights glowed brightly now. Was this smiling, genial-looking, soft-voiced creature in the chair opposite him truly the same scurrying, tight-lipped, sharp-spoken guardian of the physics labs and classrooms where Arthur had roamed so many years ago? Likely not, he thought, but was it, all the same, Professor Melville still, even though not the same? For many years Arthur had tried to work the Professor into his stories, in the way he would have liked, for Arthur had admired him enormously and would have relished, in many of those tales, a companion upon whose intelligence and competence he could have relied. Somehow or other, though, the Professor had always emerged, much to Arthur's annoyance, as more of an obstruction than an aid, holding Arthur back from his assigned tasks to whisper complex and irrelevant instructions into his ear, attempting to distract him with a thin, wily smile and alternative routes to his goal, or even, on some occasions, turning out to be the crafty intelligence behind every move of the opposition. At last, discouraged, Arthur had simply given up trying to include him in his stories, but now he was at more of a loss than ever to understand how his stories could possibly have dealt in such a way with this beaming, friendly man who rose now to greet Arthur, to take him into his very arms, like a lost son.

"Just to answer briefly some questions that must, to judge from the puzzled expression on your face, be bothering you most right now," said the Professor, leading Arthur gently to the chair next to the one he himself had been occupying, "let me tell you, first, that you have not gone unwatched these many years, through your many travels."

"Not unwatched, sir?" asked Arthur, slumping into the chair, wan and tired and unshaven and wearing clothes that had already accompanied him on a good many of those travels, up and down the Eastern seaboard.

"You can imagine my own guilt, my own sense of responsibility," continued the Professor, "when I found that my foolish asthma attack was leading to your physical disaster. With the help of Dr. Wells, that young intern whom you may remember from the health service, and my brilliant colleague Professor Kent—both of whom you will be seeing shortly—I arranged for a small electronic homing device to be implanted in the stump during the operation in which your leg was amputated. This has enabled me to keep track of your movements, your welfare, even while my own took me far off in other directions. And it has, of course, served to bring us together again, for reasons you will soon come to understand. Meanwhile, relax, we will rendezvous with friends quite soon; it's been a long day of traveling, what with the usual trouble in maneuvering the *Cinderella*—it was its usual balky self after picking me up on Ellis Island —you know, I didn't want to spring too much on you at once—and I'm sure you must be in need of some refreshment by now."

"Yes, sir," said Arthur, who, watching the Professor, was hungry but uncertain whether he could take in much more, just now, "a little something to eat maybe, and a drink of some sort, ginger ale would be just fine."

"It will be here in a moment," the Professor promised.

"In the meantime," said Arthur, "I guess I'd like to wash up just a bit. In honor of the occasion."

"No," said the Professor. The Professor himself was immaculate. In the old days, Arthur remembered, he had been a pale, unhealthy-looking man, undoubtedly brilliant but wearing the sickly pallor of one who had spent too much time cooped up indoors burrowing too intensively into tasks that were too purely intellectual. A little seedy-looking, a little harried, too, and a little . . . driven. A very promising scientist, everyone had said that about him, very promising. At the time, Arthur had idolized that look, the haunted dedication he had found on his mentor's face. But now, in view of the contrast he was faced with, he realized that what he had seen were mostly the effects of asthma and anxiety. For now the Professor appeared to be a man whose promise had been fulfilled. He was tanned, robust, and healthy-looking; his once thin face had filled out handsomely; his hair had begun to silver around the edges; he even appeared tall, though Arthur, small and skinny as ever, remembered him as being rather shorter than himself; and though he wore Western denims, they were clean and nicely pressed, and fitted his body to perfection. Elegantly tooled leather boots graced his feet, and in the chair on the other side of him, Arthur noticed, lay a gleaming white Stetson. Arthur began to think that though it might have been through an act of science that his old professor had recognized him, it was surely only through a miracle that he recognized his old professor in this . . . gentleman. Most of all was he aware, by contrast, of his own pitiful state, and of a desire, from which he had never suffered in all his years of wandering, to change it. Whereas Professor Melville now firmly forbade even the humblest beginnings of such a transformation.

"I will explain more fully later," explained the Professor, "but the important thing for now is that you remain wholly and completely yourself. No changes. Care to eat?" For as he spoke a trap door slid open in the center of the floor and a small table rose upward on a platform, bearing a delicate, unpretentious buffet selection: crackers, butter, several cheeses, slices of rare lean beef, sliced breast of chicken, olives, lettuce, a Jello mold, orange sections, milk, ginger ale, a decanter of pure water.

"I'd advise you to go lightly," said the Professor.

Motioning Arthur to remain seated, he stepped quickly to the buffet table, prepared a small plate with a variety of its offerings, poured out a glass of ginger ale, and crossed over with glass and plate to Arthur, who, more aware than ever of his tattered clothing, his stubbled face and matted hair, his filthy hands, now that he was being served by such a gracious host, could only murmur, "Yes, sir, lightly."

# Chapter 4

WHEN ARTHUR had eaten lightly and slept restlessly, dreaming over and over a dream not of adventures but simply of the many versions of his sister—now light, now dark, now tall, now small—in which at each appearance, at each transformation, she was lassoed and thrown to the ground by a tanned and balding but still athletic Professor Melville, who with sure, precise movements made a neat incision in her inner thigh, inserted a slender homing device in the opening, smoothed it closed, cut her loose, patted her rump and sent her on her way, he found the Professor standing in semidarkness at one of the saucer's portholes, beckoning for Arthur to come and join him. Together they peered into the twilight. On the horizon, the rolling yellow clouds gleamed more brightly than ever, red flames flashing across their undersides from time to time. Out of the tall rushes to one side, a dark shape glided slowly toward them. It was, Arthur saw, an ancient rust-covered garbage scow. It carried no running lights, listed sadly to starboard—looked, indeed, no longer fit for service of any sort—but on the port side of her blunt bow, Arthur saw, as the barge swung clumsily beneath them, gleamed the freshly painted silver letters of her name: *Poughkeepsie Queen*. And beneath the name, also in bright silver, but with some further dark lettering upon it which was too small for Arthur to read, in the gloom, lay a curious emblem, a question mark.

"Our friends," said Professor Melville, "but you'd best be seated again, this next is a rather tricky operation." Arthur, in his chair once more, watched the Professor open a small panel in the wall of the saucer and begin to manipulate the controls which appeared there. The saucer began to swing slowly from side to side, in a small arc, with a bouncing movement in the middle. The Professor continued to talk as he stood at the control panel. "The saucer is quite well hidden here in daylight, even to the aircraft which pass overhead, since it gives off a reflection very close to that of the oily waters beneath it. We have to be more cautious when we rendezvous with the scow, however." He slid the panel closed. The saucer dropped suddenly to the deck of the scow with a metallic clang.

What Arthur saw, when the door opened, and the landing ramp on which they stood licked gently outward through the dusk to set them down on the deck, was, first, two men scurrying about, spreading a camouflage net over the saucer, and, next, standing almost face to face with him as he stepped off the ramp, light from the open doorway to the barge's cabin area highlighting her features, smiling, her hands held out in greeting, a beautiful young woman, in whose form he saw gathered, all at once, even in that dim light, the many forms of his stories and dreams.

"These are Doctors Wells and Kent," said Professor Melville, directing Arthur's attention to the two men who, now that the net was securely spread and fastened down, stepped around from behind the saucer, "and this is your sister, Stella, perhaps the world's leading authority on gravitational phenomena."

Arthur looked, for a moment, into blue eyes that appeared to be absolutely weightless.

"This way, friends, this way," said Professor Melville, quickly shepherding them all into the hallway, "very careless of us to leave the door open here with the lights on." He pulled the door tightly closed behind them while Arthur twisted about, trying to peer over the Professor to where Stella stood silently on the other side of him, not knowing what to say, where to begin, or how. No more stories, he thought, no more stories, this was real. He wondered if that was the sort of thing he ought to try to say. It was the Professor who spoke, however.

"You go with Dr. Wells," he ordered, "there are some things that must be done immediately. Now that you're here we may as well move right along, plenty to fill you in on yet tonight." There was a delighted twinkle in his eyes. "Old scow won't stay afloat forever," he added, as he turned, ushering Stella and Kent away down the passageway, and leaving Arthur alone with Dr. Wells.

Wells led Arthur into a small room on the other side of the hall. It was only dimly lit by a single bulb; the paint, as in the hallway, was flaking from the walls, leaving large bare patches of rust showing, and it was furnished with two chromium chairs with cracked plastic seats and a Formica-topped table. There were many questions that Arthur attempted to ask, all of them prefaced with the same polite "sir" that he had used with such habitual success when thanking motorists for stopping for him, but Dr. Wells merely motioned him to one of the chairs, unbuttoned his shirt and listened to his chest, pondered what he heard, helped Arthur out of his shirt altogether so he could listen to his back and sides as well, took Arthur's blood pressure, examined his eyes, ears, nose, throat, reflexes, glands, skin, scalp, and at last ordered Arthur to get dressed again and led him out and down the passageway and opened a door for him at the end.

It was the galley. As in the hall and the examining room, only a few shreds of paint clung to the rusty walls, but here all was blackened with soot as well and the floor was littered with crumpled balls of paper, food scraps, empty tin cans and bottles, all overflowing from a garbage can wedged in behind the door. In the center was a Formica-and-chrome table, surrounded by five chairs like those in the examination room, but only Professor Melville sat there now. He looked up, past Arthur, through the open doorway, toward Dr. Wells. Dr. Wells shrugged his shoulders. Professor Melville beamed. Dr. Wells withdrew, closing the door. Arthur fumbled uncertainly into the chair that Professor Melville pointed him toward.

"I thought," began Professor Melville, "that we might have the first couple of briefings alone. There is a great deal of ground to be covered and the fewer distractions the better. Moreover, there are certain reasons for haste. For one thing, things have simply gone on long enough, there's not a reason in the world to wait any longer. Now . . ."

"Please, sir," gasped Arthur, whose mouth had been working soundlessly all this while, "my sister . . ."

"Yes indeed," said the Professor, "your sister. We shall get to her in due time. First, however . . ."

"Sir, . . ." said Arthur, still half choking.

"God dammit!" yelled Professor Melville, leaping to his feet and sending his chair clattering to the floor behind him. "You have got to stop calling me 'sir.' Immediately. No more 'sir,' understand?"

Arthur parted his lips, was ready to mutter "Yes, sir," but restrained himself at the last moment and merely nodded.

"Look," explained the Professor, picking up his chair and, calmer now, sitting back down, "you are no longer a student, Arthur. You can't even call yourself an ex-student any more. You have been wandering about for almost ten years now. Ten years! You're a *man* now, Arthur, and your life has gone absolutely nowhere."

"I know," he answered.

"Congratulations," said Professor Melville.

Chapter 5

WHAT PROFFESSOR MELVILLE went on to tell Arthur,
after this sudden outburst with its surprisingly pleasant, if
rather curious, conclusion was as follows:

He had left the University some ten years ago himself,
hard upon Arthur's own departure but in the opposite direction, taking with him only his asthma, his guilty con-
science, his stocks and bonds, and a determination to depart
forever from a field in which, while accomplishing little himself, he had inflicted damage on another human being. That,
of course, was before he understood.

He had soon settled in a small town in the Southwest,
where, at least, he thought he might do some good for his
asthma. There he had rented a tiny adobe house, far out

beyond the edges of the town itself, in a barren canyon with no trees and a sandy floor, had begun to fiddle around with leather tooling and ceramics, using as his guide a pair of elementary books on the subjects he had picked up in a tourist shop on the way there, had spent a great deal of time very pleasantly by reading all the popular novels that were available from the lending library in the town drugstore, and had watched a great many sunsets, as a man in virtual retirement might well do, especially when his canyon and his front porch face west.

There was a brief time when he occupied himself with the notion of becoming self-supporting, just for the fun of it. In a great flurry of activity he began to make belts and pots almost on a round-the-clock basis. If it worked, he thought, he might put all his securities in Arthur's name, and place them in trust for him. His idea was that he might take his products to town, and there simply trade them for his needs. But on the day when he finally went to town, lugging as many samples of his wares as he could carry in a burlap sack slung over his shoulder, the owner of the general store, where he had thought he might best do his trading, escorted him silently to a small room at the back of the store. Through the open doorway the Professor saw shelf after shelf of dusty pots and carton after carton of elegantly tooled leather belts. The shopowner was kind and neither smiled nor offered sympathy, but Professor Melville did not even have the nerve to abandon his samples in the store and instead carried them away with him, and dumped them in a dry creek bed on the way home.

What he soon discovered, however, was that though he had lost all interest in tooling leather—which had been all along tedious work for him—he still felt like making pots: if not for profit, at least for his own pleasure. That was a sort of beginning. So he went on making pots, in all sizes and shapes. He kept up with his novels and his sunsets, but gradually the house began to fill up with pots and he took to setting them all around the canyon floor as well. Such was his delight at this time that he even began, at last, to answer the letters of the one dear colleague from the university who had continued to correspond with him. He carefully avoided in these letters any discussion of the past, the university, or the sciences, and begged his colleagues to do so too. He wrote, instead, of his sunsets, his novels, his pots, while Professor Kent, on his part, spoke of movies, politics, and the weather.

When, after many years, Professor Melville began to play around with glazes, instead of shapes, their correspondence started to undergo subtle changes. Professor Kent's letters became less and less informative about events in the East, and more and more curious about happenings in the West, and when one day, after a couple of years of such activity, Professor Melville wrote a letter about a glaze which he had manufactured from the black powder derived from a meteorite he had found buried in the sand in a corner of his canyon and which had baked to such a hard finish that even when he dropped the pots to which he had applied it from considerable heights they did not break, what he received in return was not a letter but Professor Kent himself, standing on his doorstep early one morning.

What Kent explained was that over the recent years he had demonstrated quite successfully the theoretical possibility of interstellar travel at a speed that would effectively bring the time span for such travel within a reasonable human framework. Nor was there any doubt about the practical feasibility of his discovery. In fact, just such a spaceship, with just such a propulsion system as he had theorized for such travel, was already under construction. The purchase of the warehouse near the university where the project was under way, as well as of the components for the spaceship, was being financed under the auspices of a private, nonprofit foundation, known as the Poughkeepsie Institute, which Kent had provided with funds from his own pocket; from relatives, friends, and a variety of private investors who had been wheedled into putting money into a secret project that would produce both progress and profits; and from the usual vague university and government research sources. Professor Melville was welcome not only as a charter investor in the Poughkeepsie Institute but also as a scientific partner, who might well have discovered the one item which the project still lacked: a coating for the spaceship which would withstand the tremendous shock and heat of interstellar acceleration. Was Professor Melville interested?

No, Professor Melville was not interested. His friend was welcome to what remained of the glaze, which to him had been only a passing curiosity. Professor Kent took the gift that was offered him, expressed his sorrow that he could not be taking his friend along as well, and departed that same day, before evening. Professor Melville sat down on his front porch, novel in hand, to await the sunset. Tomorrow he would try a new glaze using something he had totally neglected so far, the common sand on the canyon floor.

A week later he received two letters from Professor Kent on the same day. The first announced joyously that the glaze worked, that there was just enough of it to provide a complete coating for the flying saucer which he had designed and which was already nearing completion, and that the starship was to be christened the *Cinderella* in honor of the simple black dust from which its magnificent coating had flowered. The second letter simply stated that it was all off, that interstellar flight was not, and never would be, possible.

It was at this point that Professor Melville became interested, and hastened East to rejoin his friend.

What he found when he arrived was a disconsolate physicist, a spaceship which lacked only its interior furnishings for completion—no matter, Kent assured him, the coffers of the Poughkeepsie Institute were depleted anyway—and a beautiful young woman who was introduced to him, by Kent, as the most brilliant graduate student he had ever worked with. But his face showed great pain as he said this.

"She's the one," he explained.

For she had indeed been the one who, just as the nearly finished saucer had emerged from the gigantic kiln that had been constructed for it, glazed and gleaming and looking as if it might soar away at that very moment for the most distant star, had announced her freshly completed discovery that such travel could never take place. Her proof was, to her mentor's dismay, complete and irrefutable. Working with data on the sun's gravitational pull, her specialty, in order to determine the optimal flight path and speed for the saucer's departure from the solar system, what she had discovered instead was that at the outer edges of the solar system—of, she was now able to demonstrate, any solar system— where the gravitational pull of the sun reached its farthest limits, a peculiar phenomenon occurred in which the very force of gravity itself, making a sort of final lunge before dying out, performed a hitherto unknown maneuver which she was best able to describe as "curling back in upon itself." What was thus created around the entire solar system was a continuous gravitational vortex, into which anything within a limited distance would be sucked and bound forever, and through which nothing could pass, in either direction, except light—and even that, she had found, was so radically distorted by its passage that all the star charts and all the theories of the universe which had been derived from the motion of light would now have to be revised to take this phenomenon—the Stalemate Effect, she had labeled it, though neither she nor Professor Kent found any reason to refer to it any longer—into account.

So no one could leave the solar system and no one could enter it. Man could travel to the farthest planets—to Uranus and Neptune and Pluto—but beyond that, never. What, then, was the purpose of it all? Professor Kent had built—or almost built—a remarkable starship that was too small and too swift to be of any use in mere interplanetary flight and far too delicate and sophisticated to be anything but clumsy in the primitive confines of the earth's atmosphere. How could so much come to so little?

That was precisely what Professor Melville, who had journeyed East himself with that very question in mind, was about to explain.

# Chapter 6

"B **ut my** sister?" inquired Arthur.

"Your sister," said Professor Melville, "was, needless to say, the brilliant young woman who discovered the Stalemate Effect. Shall we digress for a moment?"

"Please," said Arthur.

Professor Melville went to the door and called for Dr. Wells, who appeared shortly with a plate of bread-and-butter sandwiches, a bottle of ginger ale, and two glasses. The bread was dry and the ginger ale warm, but Arthur nibbled at the one and sipped of the other while Professor Melville digressed.

After apologizing for the fact that their provisions were running low, and that Arthur had to put up with such an unpalatable supper, he went on to tell how no one, at first, was quite certain where Stella had come from. The University had neither undergraduate transcripts nor applications nor documents of admission for her, but in the meantime her performance had been so spectacular in both classroom and lab that Professor Kent had been able to argue successfully for both her formal admission to the Graduate School of Physics and her assignment as his assistant. That she was Arthur's sister no one had suspected either, for in spite of some rather remarkable similarities of appearance she went under a different last name and it was not until Professor Melville himself, in the days following his return to the University, noted in her work a striking similarity to the unique way in which Arthur had once approached the problems of physics, that the uncovering of this relationship had begun. And once begun, where else could it end? With Stella's dedicated assistance, and much helpful footwork and record searching by Professor Kent, who badly needed an activity of this sort to take his mind off the collapse of the starship project—and who was also seeking to evade the fact that the Poughkeepsie Institute, for which he was solely responsible, was now in deep financial trouble as unpaid bills for the *Cinderella* components began to pile up—the investigation proceeded apace. Stella was not, it turned out, the child of Arthur's mother and father, but, it was soon discovered, neither was Arthur.

At this point Stella herself, in an immaculate white lab smock, entered the galley. Professor Melville smiled up at her. Arthur looked hopefully into her eyes and then suddenly knew where he had seen that impossibly light shade of blue before; for in spite of all the transformations the sister of his dreams had undergone, he now realized that there had been one constant, and that was the color of her eyes, which was identical to his own. Proof perfect: as far as he was concerned, he no longer needed the rest of the Professor's story, though he attended politely, if with more attention to the real sister than to the one being explained to him, while she seated herself quietly at the table between the two men, and sipped ginger ale from Arthur's glass, and the digression continued.

Arthur, as his foster father Arthur Hoppe, Jr., a prosperous Midwestern banker, had finally admitted when pressed by Professor Melville after several interviews, had been the infant child of an unwed mother brought into the Hoppe household when, with Mrs. Hoppe beyond childbearing age, their true son and only heir had been declared missing and presumed dead after a plane crash in the Brazilian jungles. Unfortunately, shortly after the adoption of the infant Arthur—Arthur III—Mrs. Hoppe herself had withered and soon died, so that in the ensuing confusion, for the aging Mr. Hoppe had depended greatly on his wife and now felt terribly responsible himself for the personal care and upbringing of his young namesake, Arthur III had never been formally adopted.

"Let me pause at this point," said Professor Melville, "for some brief moralizing. The fact is that in spite of your foster father's deep affection for you and your own sense of belonging to the Hoppe family tradition, you were not, so far as that relationship is concerned, going anywhere. Your final letter to Mr. Hoppe—indicative, by the way, of how guilty you felt at disappointing this family—was entirely gratuitous, asking as it did that your name be stricken from a will in which it had never been included. If anything, it almost reminded the poor, confused old man to put you in the will after all. Now, of course, it's too late."

"Dead?" asked Arthur.

"Senile," said Professor Melville. "Incontinent. Institutionalized. It was almost impossible to hold a coherent interview with him."

Nonetheless, the old man had managed to explain that, a couple of years after Arthur's entry to the household and his wife's death, a frightened young woman had come to his house one day and, finding that he was indeed Arthur Hoppe, Jr., had thrust a bundled-up infant into his arms, screaming that since he had taken her one child he might as well take her other one too, and had then fled, leaving the speechless widower standing in the doorway with a baby in his arms and a toddler tugging at his pants leg from behind. Incapable of taking the burden of another child into a life already shaken with grief and responsibility, Mr. Hoppe had arranged for her adoption, provided anonymously for her care and education, kept her at a safe distance lest by some freak coincidence she and young Arthur might meet and fall in love in ignorance of their true relationship, and only when Arthur had left the University and shown that he intended to stay away exercised his influence as a member of the Board of Trustees to have her provisionally admitted to the Graduate School.

"How's she doing?" the old man had inquired at the end of the last interview. "Very fond of that girl. She and Arthur would have made a fine team. Gone places, that pair." Professor Melville had begun to assure him that Stella had already carved out a remarkable niche for herself in the scientific world, though going places would hardly have characterized her accomplishment, but Mr. Hoppe, glassy-eyed and drooling as the attendant approached with his dinner tray, was no longer attending, and the Professor's own thoughts, for that matter, had begun to move out, toward Arthur, young

Arthur, who seemed somehow still a part of all this, though Professor Melville had not yet quite put his finger on it.

"But you did do it," said Arthur, taking Stella's hand as she laid down the glass from which she had been sipping. "You found my own sister, and brought us together." He stroked the back of her hand as he held it on the Formica table top.

"Come with me now," said Stella, "we'll take a little walk outside. I think you need some fresh air now."

"That same night," continued Professor Melville, no longer looking at either of them, "things began to fit together." He squeezed the empty ginger-ale bottle with both hands. Stella and Arthur rose, still holding hands, and started toward the galley door.

"By the next morning," he went on, holding the bottle aloft, "I had a pretty good idea of what it was all about. And what might best be done."

"We'll be right back," said Stella, opening the door.

"Arthur!" called out Professor Melville, bringing the bottle down on the table with a crash just as Stella was leading her brother out the doorway. "The digression is over."

# Chapter 7

W H A T  A R T H U R and Stella had, by way of a stroll, was warm, affectionate, solemn, intriguing, and short-lived. It strongly reminded Arthur of strange moments of aloneness along the highways, especially in the midst of heavy traffic, when a driver would spot him and slow down and angle in toward the curb, and he would go hobbling forward as quickly as he could on his crutches in order not to embarrass the motorist by causing him to hold up traffic, and in the midst of this conjunction a story would begin to form in his mind, in the presence of which everything else faded into dim unreality. Sometimes he only awoke to what was going on about him when the entire telling of the story was over, and he looked about to find himself in the midst of the scenery of a different state, and seated in the front seat of a strange car beside a person he could not recall ever having seen before.

Stella, on the other hand, he felt he had always known before, no matter what her transformations. And these, at least, were now at an end. She stood fixed and real beside him, after he had followed her down the passageway and out onto the deck and then, leaving his crutches behind, had let her help him up a narrow stairway to the open platform on top of the cabin area, where they had leaned against the rail, held hands, been embarrassed at the solemnity of their affection, and looked in vain for the stars hidden behind the swamp mist whose unpleasant odor soon set them to coughing and rubbing their eyes and starting back down again. As they returned Stella explained, with delight, how they would eventually be able to trace their true parents, for though her birth had apparently been at home and unrecorded, his had been at a proper hospital, where, as with every baby born there, his footprints had been taken. Through these he could still be identified.

"Through this," Arthur corrected, pointing at his one foot as they reentered the passageway to the galley. But he said it with a certain note of mirth in his voice.

When they entered the galley, Wells and Kent were there as well, seated on either side of Professor Melville at the table. A small blackboard sat propped up on the counter to one side. It had been marked off by chalk into three horizontal sections. In the top one a straight arrow proceeded directly from a circle marked alpha, at the left, to a circle marked omega, at the right. In the center section the alpha and omega remained where they had been, but the line capped with the arrow point wandered around a great deal, sometimes crossing its own path, sometimes going almost back to the beginning, before it got from the one to the other. There were even, Arthur noted as he sat down beside Stella at the table opposite the board, a few arrows that started out and then faded away. At the bottom was neither alpha, omega, nor arrow. Instead, the whole section was filled with a cluster of tightly packed little circles. In the center of each of these was a tiny symbol, neither an alpha nor an omega, but not until he leaned, squinting, far over the table, could Arthur see that these were question marks.

"It is already growing late," said Professor Melville, "and frankly, Arthur, there is probably very little time remaining for us. Therefore with the aid of these diagrams, and these my friends and colleagues to pick up the story wherever I falter, and without any further digressions, I would like to proceed as rapidly as possible through a discussion of how things are, and how we—and you especially, Arthur—fit into this understanding of things, and hence into the action itself. If there are any questions, please don't hesitate to speak up." Arthur, after tucking his crutches away beneath his chair, straightened up and took Stella's hand again, feeling the warm pressure of her own grip as well. The Professor, at the same time, picked up a slim white pointer, and directed Arthur's attention to the upper section of the blackboard.

"This first diagram," he explained, "is an obvious human ideal, to which we have all subscribed at one time or another, to which most still subscribe, no doubt: the beginning here, the movement sure and clear and direct, the end here. These are mere symbols, Arthur, but they are, as you must remember, infinitely extensible, and *that*"—here he paused to tap the board with his pointer—"*that* is teleology. Teleology, Arthur: the movement of life toward a distant goal. There you have it, in its most ideal form, as if directed by a divine force, which permits no digressions.

"On the other hand," he continued, shifting his pointer down now to the middle panel, which reminded Arthur—who had already been prompted to think that what the first diagram needed was an arrow going in the other direction as well if it were to illustrate the way he himself had gone, up and down along the Atlantic coast—somewhat more accurately of his own travels, more circuitous than he liked to think, dependent on the whims of unknown motorists, and sometimes involving considerable backtracking, "if that first diagram represents a teleological ideal to which few are so naïve as to subscribe, this one better indicates the nature of the teleological reality in which most of us tend to believe: so full of twists and turns, false starts and doublings back, that few can see, from its midst, either the direction or the goal. And yet most, whether or not they subscribe to a notion of divine guidance, have no doubt that we are en route, more or less. That the movement of life is indeed teleological."

"Right," whispered Arthur, who had always enjoyed Professor Melville's lectures, and was now getting back into the spirit of them again.

"No," corrected Professor Melville, waving the wand in Arthur's direction this time, "not right at all. And that is the reason we are here.

"Life has been afoot a long time now, Arthur," he went on, leaning—rather sadly, Arthur thought—on his pointer, whose end rested on the table, "and it should be reasonably obvious from a minimum of examples that we have not much gotten anywhere. If we have managed to shed most of our hair and evolve an opposable digit only to be able to button up the clothes that do the job hair once did, it can hardly be called a teleological triumph. If we have managed throughout human development to maintain with great tenacity our capacity for destroying ourselves and other creatures, for raising our children to carry on the worst as well as the best of human achievement, while not making much change in either, and for continuously extending the span of human life only to find more and more to complain of in life, there remains little evidence to suggest any sort of goal, no matter how great the distance. And if—and listen closely now, Arthur, for here is the true source of our understanding, which drew me from my retirement, as I first sensed it, and has now brought us all together here—if, I say, man has at last devised a vehicle capable of speeding him to the farthest stars, possibly into contact with other life forms and unthought-of secrets of the universe, only to find in almost the same moment that he can never escape the confines of his own solar system, nor can anyone from outside ever enter it, it does not much look as if we are going anywhere." Here Professor Melville paused for a moment, before continuing.

"Look," he snapped, rapping now sharply and many times with his pointer at the bottom panel of the board, with its diagram of many circles, each with a question mark as its nucleus, "things are what they are, whatever that is. The point is that nothing is going anywhere! Life is governed not by a principle of teleology, but by a principle of *Unteleology!*"

"Unteleology," whispered Arthur, looking sideways toward Stella, whose hand he still clasped tightly. He was less discomfited by what he realized was the momentousness of his professor's revelation—no more, in fact, than he had once been discomfited by the implications of relativity theory, or the second law of thermodynamics, when their revelations had fallen upon him from the same source—than by a nagging sense of something missing. He ought, he realized as he prepared himself for the resumption of the lecture, to have a notebook and pencil in hand.

"Throughout history," continued Professor Melville, "people have done great deeds in the belief that thereafter all would go right. They have dreamed dreams of rescuing beautiful maidens, destroying evil monsters, and living happily ever after. Given a benevolent teleology, that is the way things should go, sooner or later. Even with a malevolent goal, they might learn to side with the monsters—as many throughout history have surely done—and still live happily ever after. But when neither way works, when no matter what one does all does not go right, when what follows shows no coherent relation to what went before—save, perhaps, that it happened to the same person or the same nation—when, in short, it becomes obvious that nothing—no act, no deed, no man, no land, no nation, no program—is going anywhere, then bitterness sets in. Not, Arthur, the bitterness of lost hopes—for if the hope was no more, then there would be nothing to be bitter about—but the bitterness of disappointed hopes. For who is there who has not struggled, at least in his own life, for some sign that things were going the right way?

"And yet if there were a true teleology in operation—whether governed by the unknowable laws of a god or the immutable ones of a science—why should all this struggle be necessary? If such were indeed the case, man could relax: no matter what he did or failed to do life would roll onward toward its distant teleological goal. Why fight it? Yes, Arthur, all the individual struggles for organization and direction that ebb and flow about us in the world—the poor bastard trying to give his life meaning by collecting for his favorite charity on Wednesday evenings after work, Little-League baseball, the scholar in his den and the gamblers and financiers in theirs, Fourth of July celebrations, the compiling of the Congressional Record, State Department policy—all, *all*, if only the strugglers would realize it, give evidence, by the desperation of their attempts to provide aims and orders where none exist, that there is no teleology.

"There is only this," he said, very slowly now, gesturing almost gently toward the bottom panel of the blackboard, a kind of radiance, as Arthur saw it, suffusing his perspiring face, "only this: Unteleology. And if there is any movement at all, to this Principle of Unteleology, it is only the movement toward purposelessness."

"But," countered Arthur, releasing Stella's hand to flash his own briefly in the air, once again the bright student, eager to please and challenge his professor, "isn't that, since it's at least movement in some direction, toward some sort of goal, also a teleology?"

"You wouldn't say that," replied Professor Melville, a great calmness in his voice now, "if you knew how unsuccessful it was."

# Chapter 8

"I THINK," said Arthur, very carefully now, "that there's probably much to what you've said, but also that perhaps it's only a matter of degree. A baseball game, if I may use that humble example, is still a baseball game, even if poorly played." Arthur knew, for he had paused in his hitchhiking days to observe many a sand-lot game. "Even," he added, "if rained out." For he had also seen many boys go scurrying off to shelter in the midst of a game, while he himself continued to stand by the roadside, getting soaked through.

"Out at first!" exclaimed Professor Melville. "Many the game I was in as a boy that never was a game because we played so poorly we couldn't get anybody out, and many the older kid who sneered at us with intuitive precision and said, '*That's* not baseball.' No, Arthur, Unteleology is by no means a teleology of its own. Though there may well be events—the toppling of a government, an outbreak of mongolism, the death of a promising poet at an early age, the development of a new weapon, the burning of the last copy of a valuable manuscript—that make it appear that Unteleology is proceeding apace, there are sufficient countering events—the founding of a new government, the discovery of a hitherto unknown species of butterfly, the election of a President, the formation of a string quartet, the birth of one's first child—to make it clear that nothing, not even Unteleology, is really going anywhere.

"And as for your rained-out game, Arthur, even that is a real game only if it goes five full innings, or four and a half if the home team is winning, before the rain cancels it; otherwise it is extinguished by its own rules, and becomes nothing at all—for all practical purposes has never existed, and has no place in history, in the record books. But even that is not always successful. If a player is struck in the head by a bean ball in the top of the fifth of a game that is subsequently canceled because of rain, he may still be suffering the next day from a concussion resulting from a pitch that was never thrown in a game that was never played. Think, Arthur, of Dizzy Dean and all the other players whose careers were ruined by injuries received in those meaningless All-Star games: can any teleology explain that? And yet the people cry out 'Why? why?' Oh, the useless agony of it, Arthur, the sad useless agony expended on an attempt to find a teleological sense of meaning where no teleology exists.

"The point is, Arthur," he announced after a brief pause, "to get the whole world in tune with Unteleology." For, Professor Melville went on to explain, now that he had come to understand Unteleology—and that understanding in itself was merely the coincidental offshoot of events headed in other directions altogether, hence itself an example of purposelessness—he, like his friends here, Dr. Wells, Dr. Kent, Stella, had become remarkably at ease within his own life. It was this, and this alone, that had enabled him to draw all the discomforts of his past into a comprehensible—if meaningless—perspective: his debilitating asthma, his failure to realize his early promise as a research scientist, the incalculable damage he had inflicted on Arthur. If his life had been meant to go anywhere, if there were some scientific discovery through which he could have brought progress or meaning to human life, then all these events would have been monstrous, impossible to live with, antihuman. But the universe was neither human nor antihuman, no more than it was good or evil, god or devil: it simply *was*. It wasn't going anywhere, and neither was he, or science, or mankind. As soon as he understood this, frustration had dissolved, despair fled from him like a vampire before the rising sun, and if his asthma had not been cured as a result—why should it have been? This was simply the way things were, not a panacea— nevertheless a patina of apparent health had blossomed upon his features, a deep golden-brown tan that had suddenly appeared only after he had left the open, sun-drenched vistas of the Southwest.

And if, by some chance, he—or better yet, he interjected, Arthur, since that was the prime purpose of this gathering— were yet to accomplish anything, by virtue, for example, of an understanding of the workings of Unteleology, what better example than his own life could there be to answer Arthur's earlier question, not only of unsuccess, of lack of direction, but of the failure, even, of directionlessness?

It was well past midnight by this time. Arthur, trying to sort through the tired byways of his mind to phrase the question that would enable him to discover how *he* might "accomplish" anything as a result of his dim grasp of the workings of Unteleology, felt only the sense of numb lostness that he had once encountered, in the past, when a motorist giving him a ride in a new car had suddenly turned off the main highway and raced for many hours, at high speeds, over unknown roads, perhaps through many states, and then unceremoniously deposited him at a vacant and unmarked crossroad in the middle of the night. Professor Melville, meanwhile, had dismissed his colleagues, laid the pointer and the blackboard on the floor, and leaned now over the table toward Arthur.

"There is only this left to say," he said. "Just before dawn you will take off in the *Cinderella,* alone. It will carrry you to a parking orbit just behind a stationary communications satellite, where you will be invisible to earth trackers. You will remain there for twenty-four hours. On the following day the *Cinderella* will land you at a preselected site in a densely populated area. Your landing will, of course, be followed on radar and observed by millions, all of whom will expect whatever emerges from that remarkable craft to be a highly intelligent life form from another world. Since both the materials and the abilities of the ship far exceed present earth knowledge, there is probably little you will be able to do to convince them otherwise. But what they learn from *you,* Arthur—not so much from what you say as what you are—will soon *show* them otherwise. In your person will they experience the reality of Unteleology as they would not learn it from a thousand lectures of mine on the subject! That starship, this occupant: the Stalemate Effect itself! You, Arthur, will go forth like my son—for I feel now as if you were, indeed, my son—to help bring the world in tune with the Principle of Unteleology!"

All Arthur could bring forth was, "Tomorrow morning!"

"This very morning!" answered Professor Melville, helping Arthur out of his chair, handing him his crutches, and opening the door for him. There were, of course, problems, he explained, as he led Arthur down the hall. The financial dilemma had threatened to undermine the whole Unteleology Project. That was to be expected, of course; it was in keeping with Unteleology itself. Dr. Wells, whose true talents perhaps lay elsewhere than in medicine, had been brought in by Dr. Kent as an acquaintance whose financial contacts were invaluable. Dr. Wells had indeed raised the needed funds for the completion of the project, though perhaps in less legitimate ways than Professor Melville would have preferred: shortages in University research funds had recently come to light; private investors, growing impatient for solid evidence on the profitable scientific breakthrough Dr. Wells had promised, were contacting their banks and lawyers; Treasury agents, investigating the offices and records of the Poughkeepsie Institute, had found nothing there, less than nothing. Things were rapidly closing in. It was not possible to wait any longer.

"So sleep well, Arthur," said Professor Melville, opening the door to a small room containing a cot and little else, "tomorrow is the big day." Arthur entered the room slowly, turned about, in its center, on his crutches, surveying its emptiness.

"I'm not so sure," he said. "Maybe I'm not the right person for such a big job as this."

"Arthur," explained Professor Melville, standing in the doorway, speaking with great patience now, "what I want you to understand when you leave us is simply this: that your amputation, your depression, your wandering, your general debilitation . . . all—everything you are and have done—

even your weak grasp of what we are doing at this very moment—fits perfectly into the Unteleological structure of things and makes you, therefore, precisely the one right person to carry out this mission. When you come to understand this—as you no doubt soon will—you will feel better about yourself. And that is the important thing. From that your carrying out of your task, with its inevitable rewards, will naturally follow."

"But how?" pleaded Arthur, "how? I'm only a part-time car washer, a traveler wholly dependent on others, an inconsistent storyteller and dreamer, not even my own father's son any longer. How can such a mess as my life has been fit into anything?"

"Because, Arthur, you are yet an intelligent man and a son to make a father proud. Look, Arthur, there is little doubt that if you had continued on your original path, the outcome would have gone something like this: brilliant graduate work, unique thesis project, marvelous postdoctoral research appointment, startling discovery, endowed chair, major scientific breakthrough, Nobel Prize, contribution to humanity . . . do you hear that, Arthur? *Contribution to humanity!*"

"Yes, yes, I hear. And wouldn't that have been far better than what I've become? Oh, oh, oh," moaned Arthur, piercingly aware, for perhaps the first time, in that bare room with its dim bulb and peeling walls, of what his life had come to, "I've thrown it all away!"

"But think now, Arthur," reasoned Professor Melville, "of that Contribution to Humanity: where would it have led? At the very best, like penicillin or radio waves, it would have deluded man into thinking that life was improving, that things were going his way, that, in fact, there was somewhere to be going . . . until, of course, the furor of discovery died down, and he found that things hadn't really changed much after all: that people still died and still failed to communicate. And at the worst, naturally, you might have provided man with another one of those fantastic machines—the internal combustion engine, print, the atom . . . the list is endless—which he would shortly have turned into a weapon for the destruction of himself and his planet, all the while thinking, of course, that he was only using it to pave the way to the highest of goals."

"But," said Arthur, sitting down on the edge of the cot, "surely . . ."

"Surely," said Professor Melville, "in you—who might have done all this, and so continued to delude mankind with the belief in a teleologically structured universe, but who did not, no, I think we might even say failed, failed miserably—we see . . ."

"A flop," said Arthur.

". . . the incarnation of the Principle of Unteleology," said Professor Melville.

"But," said Arthur, looking up helplessly from where he sat, "why me?"

"Why not?" said Professor Melville.

# Chapter 9

LEFT TO himself after the Professor's departure, Arthur hobbled across the small room to make use, long and loudly, of the enameled pot in the corner, returned to his cot, lay in exhaustion upon its sagging, bare mattress, but could not sleep. In the hours since his arrival on the *Poughkeepsie Queen*, whose starboard list was echoed now in the cot beneath him, he had lost a father and gained a sister, lost an assumption and gained at least the beginnings of a new way of looking at things, lost the detachment he had once embarked upon and been reunited in unexpected ways with his past, lost the northward and earthbound direction of his usual spring pilgrimage and been provided, in its place, with a new direction altogether, and an entirely new way of going.

And little enough time left before that departure. The complications were enormous, for in that departure, he realized, he would quickly lose much of what he had only recently gained—in particular his sister, Professor Melville, and his new place among these people. But since it was his sister who had discovered the Stalemate Effect, how could he not at least lend himself to its public realization, and the potential benefits thereof? And since it was Professor Melville who had both recognized the Unteleology Principle in this and brought it now to the verge of realization, how could he once again, by deserting his responsibility, disappoint this man, his long-time mentor, who now, fondly, in his own words, looked upon him, Arthur—depended on him—as a father on a son? Arthur, gazing up at the flaking paint of the ceiling, for he had neglected to switch off the light when he lay down, saw in it the peeling away of his own years of wandering life, but beneath it all, even on the rusty metal of that ceiling, a solid something against which his years lay, but which he had not even known was there all that time: the electronic homing device by which the Professor had unerringly kept track of him throughout those years! What a kind, caring . . . even paternal act. Arthur sat suddenly up on the cot, swinging his leg down to the floor. Was it possible? Professor Melville had been young in the old days, but he, Arthur, entering the University at sixteen, had indeed been sufficiently younger for it to have been possible. Their common scientific interest, their common concern, the way they had been drawn naturally together, the way the Professor had then, and after, looked out for him, the concern, and the words, which the Professor lavished upon him now—yes, and upon Stella, too—above all the responsibility which the Professor was now handing him, for the completion of his own work, what other conclusion was possible than that the

Professor was—though he could not, after all this time, admit it—his father? And Stella's! Arthur pulled his shoe back on, grabbed his crutches from beneath the cot, and hurried to the door. Not, as much as he would have liked to share this exciting discovery with, at least, Stella, to wake anyone, for dawn—the moment of his departure to fulfill his father's dreams—was only an hour or so off. But, as he had dined only on bread and ginger ale since boarding the *Poughkeepsie Queen*, because he was suddenly very hungry.

Tired, excited, suddenly animated by his hunger, he was not, as he hurried out into the passageway, quite prepared, as he turned toward the galley door at the end of the hall, for the steepness of the scow's list, but stumbled forward as he set his crutches down on the unexpected angle of the floor, struggled to regain his balance, dropped one crutch altogether and lurched across the hall and into a door, which sprang open as he thudded into it, letting him fall forward, to the floor, inside a cabin much like the one he had just left, with its peeling walls lit by a single dim bulb, except that there was a much larger bed in this room, a real bed and not a cot, and in it, Arthur saw as he sat up dazed on the floor, were Professor Melville and, trying to pull the sheet up over her naked body, Stella.

It was all Arthur could do to mutter the word that was flooding through his mind: "Incest!"

"Arthur," cried Stella, sitting suddenly up in the bed, the sheet half draped around her, one breast still exposed, "what are you talking about?"

"Him," said Arthur, pointing across the bed to where Professor Melville was standing, pulling up his pants. "He's our father." Stella twisted around to look at the Professor; Arthur bent his head down into his hand, unable to look at either of them; Professor Melville, struggling now to get his arms into his shirtsleeves, looked sharply across at Arthur.

"What in the world are you talking about, Arthur?"

"It all adds up," said Arthur, still refusing to look up, "and you even called me your son."

"It's not true, is it?" cried Stella. Arthur, looking up as she spoke, saw tears in her eyes, the tension in her hands as she clutched fearfully at the sheet.

"It's nonsense," said Professor Melville. "Of course I referred to you as my son, but that was only metaphorical, the way"—he was now fully dressed and bending over Arthur, to help him up—"I have always felt about you, especially since I felt responsible for your unfortunate accident. I am *as* fond of you, Arthur, *as if* you were my son. That's all. Except that I hoped you might also be fond of me." He brought Arthur both his crutches, patted him on the shoulder, half a caress, half an attempt to brush off any debris from the floor that might have clung to Arthur's already tattered clothing.

"Still and all, you had no right," said Arthur. "She's my sister."

"Oh, Arthur," cried Stella, "that's not fair."

"Unfortunately," said Professor Melville, "that's not true either. The story that I told you both, and that you both believed in so happily, is basically true, except for the part about the woman bringing Stella to the Hoppe household. In his senile muttering, Arthur Hoppe, Jr., let slip the fact he had managed to keep secret all these years: namely, that Stella is the illegitimate child of his own niece, given over, after the niece's death in childbirth, to be cared for as already described. Old Hoppe only wanted to protect both the child and the family name, just as my sole purpose in this slight deception was only to protect the two of you from getting so

**59**

involved in this brief time as to endanger our success. Unfortunately, my idea seems to have backfired."

"Indeed it has," claimed Arthur, trying to shrug off the professorial hand that was guiding him out the doorway and turning back to face the lovely woman, suddenly no longer his sister, on the bed. "Stella, I love you!"

"Oh, Arthur," she called, jumping up on the bed now, wrapped in her white sheet, but the Professor closed the door on this vision, ordering her as he did so to get dressed and come outside quickly, and led Arthur hurriedly down the passageway and onto the open deck of the scow, where, in the dim gray light that was beginning to filter through the sky already, Arthur could make out Wells and Kent busily removing the camouflage net from the saucer. The door of the saucer was open: a soft yellow light glowed in its interior and the tip of the landing ramp rested on the deck almost directly in front of Arthur.

"My god," said Arthur, very softly, suddenly aware that, not even knowing his own true wishes in the matter, he was about to embark on an unsolicited ride that would end with his descent from space to an audience of millions, "you're deadly serious about this."

"No, Arthur," answered Professor Melville, "not deadly serious. In fact, just barely serious enough to have gone along this far with a scheme based on the assumption that nothing gets us anywhere, and certainly not serious enough not to have felt that it might be quite as frivolous and foolish as anything else. If we had been deadly serious, we could have gotten the university or the government or private business to sponsor this affair. But the deadly serious, my young friend, are another sort altogether. If you haven't met them so far, undoubtedly you will soon. They are so serious about what they want to do that they let nothing stand in their way, turn everything to their own use. They are so serious that they can't see any other way for things to be but their way. They are so serious that they think they know what's best for absolutely everyone. And when they come and say to you, 'We're only doing this for your own good,' that's deadly, Arthur, that's deadly serious. As for us, we have found a gimmick—which, so far as I can determine, is about as much as anyone has, whether it's a great idea or a new car or a sudden passion. The point is that it is what it is, and you do what you can with it. In our case we have the world's fastest and most useless starship, we have the possibility that we might produce some interesting results, we have a reasonable certainty that we aren't likely to do any harm, we have you, and, well, as I have said before, why not?"

Why not, indeed, for even as Professor Melville spoke he led Arthur forward onto the landing ramp, which now rose slowly from the deck and paused, at the level of the Professor's shoulder, ready to withdraw into the saucer. Wells and Kent stood silently on either side of the ramp, their hands raised in farewell. Stella appeared behind the Professor, in the open doorway from the cabins, unsmiling, not dressed as ordered but still wrapped in her white sheet.

"Bon voyage, Arthur," said Professor Melville, raising his hand also. "Remember: what you do you do for the best, for all of us."

"Sir," said Arthur, "what about the homing device in my leg?"

"It's still there, of course," answered the Professor, "it seemed unnecessary to inflict another operation on you for its removal. But naturally we will be able to follow your fate from this time on through the public news media. I have the tracking device here in my pocket, as always, however, and you may have it, if you want, to dispose of as you see fit. But no more 'sirs,' Arthur. You're on your own now."

"Thank you," said Arthur, "sir." Propping his crutches very carefully on either side of him, he knelt down on the tip of the ramp and took the small metal box from the hand that Professor Melville extended to him. Raising himself back up on his crutches, he balanced the device in his own hand for a moment and then, with a gentle, sweeping gesture, tossed it out over the Professor's head to Stella, who caught it in the folds of her sheet and held it tightly to her breast. The ramp began its smooth withdrawal into the doorway of the saucer. Arthur, riding solemnly with it, smiling wanly, as the first rays of the morning sun broke through the mist at the eastern edge of the Jersey swamps, as Professor Melville and his two colleagues backed quickly away toward the cabin, and as Stella, still standing in the doorway, raised her bare arm aloft toward him, clutching the tracking device in her fist, saw, for the first time, as he turned now to enter the *Cinderella*, the silver symbol inscribed over the starship's doorway, and the words inscribed within it, thusly:

# PART II

# The Middle

# Chapter 10

IN VIOLATION of the laws of the state, the nation, and common sense, Arthur stood, propped on his crutches, with his right fist, thumb extended, raised out before him at shoulder height, in the loose gravel at the edge of the westbound lane of the Jersey Turnpike. A steady stream of cars, headlights glaring, raced by him through the night, rattling the pebbles at his feet and filling the air about him with a fine dust that settled in his clothes, his eyes, and his hair. The full moon, which, when he first took up this solitary stance, had been rising hugely bright through the dull mist that huddled along the horizon to his left, now stood directly over his head, and this he took as an indication that a good many hours had passed since he had resumed his old—no, he realized, not really so old as that: it just seemed to have come from a different era—roadside position. Never in his life had he waited so long, on any highway, in any state, at any time of day or night, without getting a ride.

For many, many years he had been accustomed to thinking of himself as a very patient man, one with nowhere special to go, and in no special hurry to get there. And never in all those years had traffic remained so aloof. Now, however, now that he had somewhere to go, and now that he was in something of a hurry to be getting there, now, of all times, did car after car after car race by him through the darkness, failing to acknowledge his presence by so much as the dimming of a headlight. He wanted to grind the tips of his crutches in the gravel and cry out impatiently to every set of flashing lights that glared so painfully in his eyes, "Why? Why?" But he did not, for he was afraid that he already knew the answer, and he did not want to hear it echoed back at him in this friendless place.

Neither was he secure, any more, in the fact that he had descended to such an arbitrary, dependent, and earthbound mode of transportation once again. It was neither the future that Professor Melville had predicted for him nor the one he had envisioned for himself when, three days before, he had rushed to open one of the portholes as the *Cinderella* dipped and hovered in the dawn skies over the Jersey swamps, as if hesitating whether to go on or to give it all up there, had seen in the thin mist below a pair of blue patrol boats, searchlights flickering ahead of them, edging through narrow channels in the direction of the *Poughkeepsie Queen,* and then had been flipped back into his seat, as the saucer tilted heavenward, and been held tightly there by enormous forces as it accelerated rapidly, and had soared away upward through the clouds and toward the stars, or so it seemed. Having risen so high, and so fast, he was not at all sure what it was, now, that he had come down to, and been left standing in the middle of, unattended to, and in the dark.

From the heights of that earlier day, safely ensconced, as promised, behind a small stationary satellite, which stretched out metal arms on many sides, as if to shield him from the earth's view, and yet far enough behind it so that it did not itself block out more than a small portion of his view of the earth, Arthur, leaving his seat to float gently over to the port-hole that opened once again to his touch, saw, with surprising clarity, where it was that he stood today. Below him, far below, and brightly lit by the morning sun, lay the soft tones —the grays, the browns, the greens—of a major segment of the Eastern coastline of the United States, from, roughly, the lower edge of Massachusetts to the upper half of the Florida peninsula. Its inlets, its extrusions, all the familiar configurations that Arthur had come to know so well during his decade of semiannual wanderings along its edge, were all so clearly visible that he could not resist pointing, with the tip of the crutch that floated weightlessly beside him in the zero gravity of the saucer, at the very spot from which he had just risen. To one side, the right, stretched the sparkling slate blue of the Atlantic; to his left, no doubt, stood the great land mass of the North American continent, its rivers, moun-tains, fields, forests, cities. But whatever there was of all that, that he might have seen, from his small moving point in space that was not going anywhere, but was staying right there above the same spot on earth, was shrouded beneath a heavy cover of clouds that, as, weightless in time as well as in space, he let the day go by, crept steadily eastward, slowly blotting from view the small corner of the Gulf that was barely visible to him and the Carolinas and Chesapeake Bay and Long Island and the great hook of Cape Cod, the tip of which was just out of sight beyond the curve that terminated his view, and then spreading out over the ocean as well, until all that he could see, as the day drew gradually to a close, was either blue or white. Aside from the blackness of all space about him.

Not a sound was forthcoming, all that while, from the saucer's communications system that had once spoken so firmly to him; not a morsel, as he drifted back to his chair and belted himself in and tucked his crutches firmly underneath, lest they wander away from him in the night, from that lovely buffet which only the day before—only the day before!—had provided him with such a pleasant, if scanty, repast; not a word or a sign of hope or encouragement, or the slightest indication of what he might best say to the waiting millions when, with the next dawn, the *Cinderella*'s motors came rumbling to life again and Arthur clung tightly to the arms of his chair and the saucer began to move downward in the great, slow sweeps that were not likely to escape detection through the uncoiling spiral that would bring it back to the planet below.

The *Cinderella* returned to Earth like a dream, but a dream canted at a slight angle. To Arthur, who had slept a dreamless sleep, it seemed as if he were being set down more gently than he had ever been set down before, and yet, when it was all over, and the *Cinderella*'s great motors fell silent, and nothing either moved or gave off sounds any more, it was still as if the journey were not quite over, the landing not altogether complete, for Arthur, gravity-bound once more, sat tilted sharply back into his seat as a result of the curious angle at which the saucer had come to a rest. One side of the saucer—the "front side," to Arthur's way of thinking, because it was the side where the door was—tilted upward at a considerable angle, while the opposite side, in the center of which was Arthur's chair, angled downward at the same pitch. For Arthur, held firmly back in his chair by this unexpected lapse from the horizontal, it was, for a long time, easier to remain there, seat belt unfastened now and crutches pulled out from under the seat and laid in readiness across his lap, for the moment when the door would open and it would be necessary for him to rise and make his way across the steep slant of the floor and out into the daylight to the waiting throng.

Thus did he sit and wait, rather than make the enormous effort called for to lift himself out of the seat, and struggle clumsily uphill, to a door that was not yet opened to him. Neither did the saucer show any inclination to move: the door remained closed, the motor silent, the portholes tightly shut, and the interior, as it had been since the moment they left the night and their orbit, brightly lit by both the deep yellow glow of indirect lighting and the ring of blue light that circled the ceiling, over Arthur's head. Nor was there any sound from outside, to indicate that an anxious crowd had gathered: no rising hum of voices, no thumping at the hull of the saucer, though all of that, Arthur realized, might have been because the mob was held in check by its leaders, or because of the solid, soundproof construction of the starship. There was only, from time to time, as Arthur sat, almost lay back, there still, a sudden, for the most part nearly imperceptible . . . shift downward along the angle at which the saucer lay, as if the *Cinderella*, not quite satisfied with its landing, was attempting to slide, without being noticed, into something of a firmer, fuller contact with the earth. Some of these, as the day wore on, seemed to Arthur to be of increasing duration, or length, he was unsure which was the proper term; but whatever it was that the saucer was about here, he felt it was succeeding. There was nothing else.

What there was, Arthur realized, was a steadily growing

sense of hunger within himself. That the door did not open Arthur could understand: it was reasonable, was it not, to assume that Professor Melville had wanted to allow sufficient time for a crowd to gather, for the radio and television networks to haul in their equipment and set it up, perhaps even for certain important personages to arrive, and so had set the mechanism of the door to open only after the necessary hours for all this to take place had passed. That the windows did not open either—would not open, Arthur found, when at last he hauled himself awkwardly up and made a clumsy circuit of the saucer, trying every porthole with equal lack of success, before returning to sink back heavily into his chair again —could also be explained on the basis that, though this unfortunately prevented him from seeing out, it also prevented those on the outside from seeing in, and so greatly enhanced the element of suspense, the climax of his ultimate appearance. That he had not been fed in orbit Arthur could also understand, for perhaps there had not been time in the hasty final outfitting of the ship to equip it for feeding its occupant in a weightless environment, and Arthur was just as happy not to have had to cope with sandwiches and condiments and silverware floating randomly about the cabin. That he was still not being fed, however, was far less to his liking: surely this was not what the Professor wanted. He thought of the small provisions—slivers from that fine buffet, bread, warm ginger ale—that had been all that was proffered to him; he thought sadly of the fine delicacy that, after all, Professor Melville had kept for himself and saw the last, hopeful arc of his own hand as it went out to Stella; he thought, lastly, that in addition to being hungry, he was possessed by a sudden and most uncomfortable urge to relieve himself. Here too, so far as he could see, no facilities had been provided aboard the *Cinderella*.

Here, however, Arthur, unlike Professor Melville, could not wait. Could he permit his first statement to the waiting crowd to be, "I have to go to the bathroom"? He eased himself out of his chair, hobbled around behind it, and there, in that lowest angle of the saucer's floor, where all that was liquid was bound to gather anyway, relieved himself. As he turned from doing so, he saw that the panel in the center of the floor had slid open while he was looking away, and that now the buffet table was beginning to rise through the opening there. On it, Arthur saw, was much the same selection from which the Professor had fed himself earlier, except that there was very little remaining, and what was there had been rather thoroughly picked over—the lettuce was wilted, the Jello melted, only scraps of meat remained, the bottles were empty—and, as the table rose upward, what few things were left on it succumbed to the angle at which the saucer lay, tumbled from the table top, and went rolling quickly past Arthur and into the small puddle he had left behind him.

Beyond the table, though, toward which, grasping his crutches, he had started as soon as he noticed the opening in the saucer's floor, he now saw that the door was open, and heard the gentle whirr of the ramp as it slid outward from the niche in which it rested at the base of the door. Neither the ramp nor the long-awaited, and awaiting, crowd, however, was visible to Arthur, for, at the angle at which the *Cinderella* lay, all he could see through the doorway was a rectangular section of sky, filled with spring thunderclouds just in the process of breaking up, patches of blue here and there, the pinkish cast of early evening, and, as a gentle breeze swept into the saucer, and around Arthur, gradually making his way uphill, doorward, pulling himself from one chair to the next, the smell of newly fallen rain.

What Arthur found, when at last he pulled himself up

into the doorway, and tucked his crutches under his arms, and moved boldly forward onto the landing ramp, looking expectantly about, was that the *Cinderella* lay almost up to its doorway now in the oily green slime of a swamp, and that the landing ramp, across which he quickly scurried, stretched from the starship to the rain-wet, soggy, but still firm ground of a gently sloping pasture. Even as he stepped from the ramp, he saw the ship slide yet a little more into the swamp, the first traces of that thick muck that spread out around and far behind the ship, to disappear among dried clusters of spiky weeds, beginning to ooze through its still-open doorway. Beside Arthur, as he stood in the pasture and watched the *Cinderella* sink slowly out of sight into the green-and-black depths of the swamp, stood three brown cows, facing the same way he was, their rumps to the setting sun. As far as Arthur could tell from the clouds, the swamp, the yellow haze that hung out on it, the smell, the vegetation—for Arthur was an experienced and knowledgeable traveler—it was still springtime, and he was once again in New Jersey.

# Chapter 11

W H E N  T H E  *Cinderella* was gone, and Arthur had waved
farewell to the question-mark insignia emblazoned over its
door, which was the last portion of the saucer visible before
it sank quite out of sight beneath the surface of the swamp,
he turned and followed the three brown cows, who led him,
through the last light of the evening, up over the pasture,
away from the swamp, through bushes and over small creeks
and along the soggy rolling ground, into which his crutches
continually sank, so that he had to pause and jerk them free,
until at last, as darkness fell, they left him completely behind,
and he was forced to find his own way, slogging along through
muddy cow paths, blundering into fences and clusters of
brush, trying to hold to the higher ground lest he wander

down into the swamp himself, slipping, time and again, on the treacherous little hillsides, caught there in the open and alone by what seemed to be almost hourly rainfalls throughout the night. At dawn he came to a narrow, rutted country lane, unfit for any vehicle. At noon he encountered three small boys, picnicking by its side, who were frightened off by his approach, but left him an excellent collection of hard-boiled eggs. At nightfall he found an empty barn, and there he slept, on through most of the following day. When he awoke late on that third day, he finished the last of his hard-boiled eggs, stepped out into the pleasant spring evening, and saw, from the small rise where the barn was situated, that at no great distance before him lay the broad, flowing stream of the New Jersey Turnpike, whereon, as darkness fell once more, he shortly took up his accustomed stance.

That he was not having his customary good fortune at the roadside, however, did not occur to him at once, for he was much preoccupied, as he stood there with first one hand extended, thumb out, and then the other, the moon rising over his muddy, disarrayed shape and the traffic passing him steadily by, with the question of what had happened. Where, he wanted to know, was the welcoming throng, the attention of the news media, the audience of millions? How had it happened that the landing, and his reception, had not worked out as Professor Melville had planned? When, if ever, would all go right, at last? What, he also began to pose, ought he to do now, but he realized as he stood there, the moon in its speedy orbit edging high over his head, dust drifting through his tangled hair and into the corners of his eyes, and car after car speeding past him, as, he was abruptly aware, they had never done before, ever, that he had, in effect, already answered that question. There he was, with his thumb pointing, for the first time, West. And his whole stance was a commitment, he knew, in the direction of the University, to which, perhaps, Professor Melville, or at least Doctors Wells or Kent, and maybe, who knows, Stella, had returned by now: where, perhaps, they anxiously awaited him, with the answers to his questions, and his needs.

The catalogue of needs that he compiled as he stood there in the swirling roadside gravel included Stella, food and rest, a good cleanup, comfort and affection, a father, and information—on, for example, what he ought to do next, why things had gone the way they had, and how, if at all, the Professor's goals might yet be fulfilled. At the head of his list of needs, however, was the need for a ride, for he had a good many states to traverse before reaching that one in the Midwest where he might find the rest of his needs attended to. He considered making a collect long-distance call to Professor Melville or one of the others, but what, he wondered, would he do if none of them was there, and how would he feel if one of them was there but refused to accept the collect charges on his call, and what, too, if by the mere act of calling he were to reveal his name and location to the wrong individual and so, in some way he did not understand, spoil the Professor's plans?

He preferred to ride. But though he had had, over the years, great success in traveling north and south, and even, in the more recent past, up and down, this was his first venture on an east-west axis, and it was a failure. All through the night and into the next day the fine, smooth late-model cars in which he had been accustomed to ride—chauffered toward Maine or Florida by a dapper, middle-aged traveling salesman or a pair of vacationing college boys or a white-haired grandmother or even, now and then, a young couple with a child seated between them—continued to pass him by. Even the older cars and the trucks, for which he had never had to wait before, gave no sign of slowing for him. Only when, for the first time since he had taken up his position there, a car, not a terribly old one at that, shuddered and paused as it passed him, skittered about hesitantly for some yards on the highway, and then wobbled unsteadily to the shoulder of the road where he found, when he hobbled forward to meet it, that it was not he but a blowout that had brought it to a halt, did he discover where his traveling salvation lay.

Among these mechanical cripples, which he found, now that it had been called to his attention, lined the highways on all sides and at what seemed to be fairly regular intervals, he was able to make his way westward. For the effort of assisting at the changing of a tire, or a minimal amount of tinkering around beneath the hood, he was able to instill a sufficient sense of obligation in the driver of the disabled vehicle, who remained immaculate while he only dirtied himself further, to assure himself of a ride, in most cases. Only once was he denied outright, by the driver of a trailer truck who took one look at Arthur when they had finished a task for which the driver's own two hands had been insufficient and said, as he climbed up into his cab, "Yer a mess. Go away." On such occasions as Arthur was unable to prod a silent engine back into motion again, he shrugged his shoulders and went hobbling on down the highway, toward the next cripple.

His first ride was with the farmer in the recent Chevrolet whose tire he changed, a pleasant, rust-colored little man who had been to visit his married children in the east and now drove Arthur westward across the entire state of Pennsylvania at twenty miles per hour. They were stopped on several occasions by police cars, who either ticketed the old man for driving below the posted minimum speed or ordered him to use the less heavily traveled roads, but he stuck relentlessly to the turnpike, shared with Arthur a large sack filled with olives and pickle slices and chicken-salad sandwiches with the crusts trimmed off, and listened patiently to what Arthur had to say to him. For perhaps the first time in a vehicle with a stranger, Arthur was not telling one of his stories. It had occurred to him, while changing the tire, that even though the venture with the saucer had turned out badly, there were still perhaps other ways for him to assist in the fulfillment of Professor Melville's goal. Perhaps, he thought, the best thing, in the present circumstances, was simply to try to convey the Professor's idea to whomever he met in the course of his daily existence, letting loose its benevolent influence on at least those few individuals, that they might be set at ease in their lives. Therefore as they crept across the great length of the Commonwealth of Pennsylvania, Arthur recited, to the best of his recall and ability, but omitting all mention of the starship, lest it cause undue suspicion, the theory of Unteleology. When he finished, Pittsburgh was looming into view, but it was not till they were nearly at the Ohio border that the farmer responded, first bringing his car to a gentle stop on the side of the highway.

"That so?" he said, handing Arthur the sack that lay on the front seat between them. "Here, take these sandwiches. This's as far as I go."

His next ride was with a young minister in an old car with a broken fan belt, which Arthur tediously wired together in the hopes that it might last a few miles more. The minister's gratitude was, however, limited to basic transportation, for as soon as they were on their way he turned to Arthur, who was already beginning to formulate some phrases on the question of divine guidance through which he felt the subject might best be broached to a man of the cloth, and asked him not to talk, please, for he was accustomed to working out in his mind, as he drove, ideas for his next sermon. In rapid succession, Arthur rode with a teenage girl obviously too young to be legally driving and too inexperienced to know what a jack was; with a drunken men's-wear salesman who had stopped to urinate and lost his keys in the grass at the roadside; and with an old giant of a man in a dump truck filled with used automobile tires, among which Arthur scrambled for half an hour till he found one of a passable size and condition to replace the blown-out front tire of the truck. Inside the cab, however, it turned out to be far too noisy, as they rattled on into the heart of Ohio, to allow any conversation.

His next ride, a considerably longer one, was with a bus-load of baseball players from a small college in central Ohio who were on their way to play at a similar college in Indiana. They had a double-header scheduled for the following day. When Arthur came across them, they were plunged into a deep gloom, for not only were they stranded on the side of the highway, while their driver tinkered ineffectually with an engine wholly unfamiliar to him, but it was raining steadily, and they were listening, on their portable radios, to the dismal weather forecasts for the morrow. When Arthur had successfully removed the foreign substance that was clogging up the carburetor, it turned out that there was not an extra seat available for him on the bus. He was content, however, as they set out across the farmlands of western Ohio, to take up a position beside the driver, which left him standing, as he turned to speak to the young men in their identical blue and gold jackets, like a teacher in front of a classroom. He lectured with such obvious care, both for his subject and his audience, that the ballplayers could not help putting down their magazines and textbooks, turning off their portable radios, jostling their neighbors into wakefulness, and attending to what he said with an equal show of care. He told them, in the best words that he could muster up, which were mostly Professor Melville's, everything that he knew about Unteleology: about what it was and about how it worked and how, sometimes, according to its very nature, it failed to work, and about the benefits of bringing mankind in tune with it. He saved for the very last his favorite part, the analogy with the baseball game.

"That," he concluded, "is just the way it is, and there is no sense in asking 'Why?'—a question which is merely the product of a serious misconception of how the universe works—when for every 'Why?' there is a 'Why not?,' as only Unteleology effectively explains." At this point the coach, a brown-suited man with a great belly and a well-tanned bald head, who had been sitting in the back row with the newspaper held in front of his face all this while, carefully folded the paper on his lap and looked down the length of the bus toward Arthur.

"That," the coach said, "is the most fantastic thing I have ever heard." He paused to unwrap a fat cigar and poke it into the corner of his mouth before continuing. "Whattaya trying to do, say that this game isn't important? Baseball's as important as eating or sleeping to these boys; in fact, they *do* eat and sleep baseball. It means everything for them to play the game right and to win, and that's the way it'll be if they practice and have the right attitude and play their very best. They'll win. This is a fine team, I want ya to know. Why should it be any other way, huh? Why?"

The answer to the coach's question hung, unspoken, a question itself, in the narrow aisle of the bus, with the silent players turned toward it from either side and Arthur and the coach looking at it from opposite ends. The coach finally struck the match he had been holding in his hand for some time, and lit his cigar.

"What if," said Arthur, "your leading hitter stumbled rounding third base with the tying run, and was thrown out by ten feet?"

"Whattaya talking about?" cried the coach, blowing great clouds of cigar smoke down the aisle. "Whattaya trying to do, mess up my boys' minds? Ya'll ruin everything. Stop the bus! Get this guy outa here!"

"Listen," said one of the young ballplayers, reaching over, as the bus slowed and pulled to the side of the road, to tap his teammate across the aisle on the knee, "you know the way those lazy flies come drifting out to center field, way high up and easy-like? Well, sometimes I think I'd just like to stand there and watch them go over, you know?" Arthur, clumping down the steps, paused in his descent from the bus to watch the boy across the aisle rise violently from his seat and grab the center fielder by the front of his jacket.

"For chrissake," he screamed in his teammate's face as he shook him about in his seat and other ballplayers leapt up to converge on the two of them, "why?"

# Chapter 12

I T W A S still raining when Arthur left the bus, and the bus left Arthur behind, and it continued to rain all that evening and through the night and on into the following day, as Arthur found one crippled vehicle after another to carry him on westward, bit by bit. He thought, as Indiana fell behind him, of how those young and pleasant-looking baseball players would be sitting disconsolately in the visitors' dugout, heads hanging, staring at the rain-soaked field, perhaps wondering why they had come so far only to look at the puddles along the first-base line, and he wished that what he had tried to say to them could have been, as he had hoped, some help. Whether the failure of Unteleology to work its benevolent effects was a result of the inadequacy of the theory, of his insufficiency as a teacher, or of the utter futility of words, mere words, whether his or the Professor's, to do much of anything, he did not know, but after a few more unsuccessful ventures—one with a retired English teacher who sold laboratory equipment to high schools, did not understand why her battery cables had to be attached firmly, and tried to show Arthur by extensive quotation how each of his arguments had been foreseen and answered in the Old Testament; another with a sandy-haired, crew-cut young man who claimed to be driving a stolen car, enlisted Arthur's assistance for a rapid changing of the license plates, and later responded to each of Arthur's comments by chanting "Yeah, yeah" with a gleefully blank expression on his face—Arthur abandoned altogether his attempt to explain Unteleology and was satisfied to ride in silence, neither telling stories nor enunciating theories, until his destination was reached.

Inasmuch as Arthur arrived on the University campus at mid-morning, it took him very little time to learn from the secretary of the Dean of the Graduate School, who did not, of course, know Arthur but was bubbling over with gossip, that Dr. Wells had dropped out of sight many years ago after failing his medical exams for the third time, but was rumored to be performing illegal operations on wealthy patients for exorbitant fees; that only that morning a picture postcard had arrived from Bogotá carrying on one side a picture of an Indian harvesting coffee beans and, on the other, a message from Professor Kent, announcing his resignation from the faculty; that Professor Melville, currently the University's most highly publicized ex-faculty member, with the possible exception of an aging appeals-court judge who was being sued in a local court on paternity charges, was now in the federal penitentiary in New York, as good as convicted on charges of embezzlement of private, state, and federal funds; and that Stella was remembered with great fondness. All had been disappointed when she suddenly abandoned an obviously brilliant science career in the midst of her graduate work. Where was she and what was she doing these days, anyway?

Arthur allowed as how he did not know, but he imagined to himself, as he hobbled down the steps of the administration building, and across the mall among students in commencement-day robes scurrying toward the stadium, that wherever she was, she held firmly in her hand the small tracking device that was tuned in to the homing mechanism in his stump and so moved gradually toward him, still dressed in white. But could he simply stand and wait for her? Where? And for how long? In a corner booth he found Dr. Wells's name listed in the telephone book, under "Financial Counseling," since he recalled that money, rather than medicine, was where Professor Melville had suggested his talents lay, in the yellow pages. When he dialed the number, Dr. Wells himself answered on the first ring, expressed both surprise and pleasure at hearing from Arthur, and immediately urged Arthur to stay away from him, for the time being. Yes, he informed Arthur, the police had indeed arrived soon after the *Cinderella*'s take-off, but it was only Melville they wanted since, in the end, none of the others had any formal or legal connection with the now-defunct Poughkeepsie Institute. He, Wells, had after all only been a financial go-between, Kent merely a technical adviser, Stella . . . he was not sure what Stella's relationship had been. It was certain, however, that Melville, as the Institute's sole officer, director, and employee, however unpaid, would receive a lengthy sentence for misappropriation of funds. No, he did not know why the *Cinderella* had come back to a landing in the Jersey swamps; he was not privy to all of Melville's plans. He only knew that if things had gone on a little longer, and a little better, they would all have been rather more deeply involved in the legal responsibility of the Poughkeepsie Institute, for he had a drawer full of stock certificates made out in the Institute's name, and it had been intended that each of them would receive a significant number of shares, and that the rest would be put out as a public offering. He supposed he ought to get rid of those. He also supposed that it might be best if Arthur, whose precise connection with Melville's venture was not altogether clear, and was perhaps also unfinished, did not appear in person at the offices of Wells Investment Counseling. In the meantime, did Arthur need any money?

"No," said Arthur sadly as he reached up to hang up the phone, "or maybe yes, a little," and he named the intersection where the telephone booth was.

All through the rest of the spring and on into the first few days of the summer, Arthur, living off the small dole which Dr. Kent brought him every couple of days at noon at the same intersection, slept at the Gospel Mission, ate White Castle hamburgers several times a day, and spent most of his waking hours on a green wooden bench in a small park adjacent to the University where he waited patiently for his homing device to bring his Stella home, at last, to him. Gradually, however, Arthur, who was not used to doing nothing, and waiting, but had long been accustomed either to traveling or to working when he was not traveling, grew impatient with his inactivity. Perhaps, he reasoned, Stella was indeed heading toward him, but would she not take notice at once, thanks to the homing device, of any shift in his location? Given his usual rate of travel, there was, so far as he could see, no reason why she should have any trouble catching up with him, wherever he went. That there was nothing further to be accomplished around the University he was certain; at best he was, so long as he remained here, only a continuing personal, business, and financial embarrassment to Dr. Wells. On the other hand, there was Professor Melville, almost a father to him at one time, now equally hapless and alone—already, Wells had reported to him at their last Monday meeting, brought swiftly to trial, found guilty without hesitation, speedily sentenced, and immediately incarcerated in the federal penitentiary in New York, to begin serving the several decades of his prison term—from whom there might yet be some solace, advice, or, at the very least, information, about the fate of this entire venture, and all involved in it, to be gained.

With this in mind, and noticing a young man parked at the nearby curb who was having difficulty getting his small sports car started, Arthur pulled his crutches out from under the bench, where he had stowed them so that the children running through the little park wouldn't trip over them, and rose up, and hobbled straight forward, ignoring the small sign that advised him to keep off the grass, and so at midday at the begining of the last week of June set out upon the road once more. Once again, he found, no one stopped for him when he tried to hitchhike, and it was only those for whom he stopped, the cripples of the highway, who carried him forward. He did not meet any more athletic teams on his way East, and only once, briefly, did he attempt another exposition of Unteleology, but that was abruptly halted at a traffic light in Alton, Illinois, when the woman who was driving interrupted Arthur to tell him that she would be happy to buy copies of whatever literature he was peddling but that if he intended to continue on towards Peoria with her, it was absolutely necessary that he terminate his spiel at once.

He also rode with a potbellied, balding little man whose back seat was packed tight with sample cases and who offered to take him to Florida and have him fitted with a prosthetic leg and promised to set him up in a nice apartment near the beach, where they could both have lots of fun, but Arthur declined, saying that he had something important to do in the East and that he had already seen enough of Florida in his younger traveling days. The man laughed when Arthur said "younger" and asked Arthur how "old" he was now. When Arthur answered with his honest thirty, the man was flabbergasted, and told Arthur that he looked more like just a college kid.

Arthur, who felt that his collegiate education was ages behind him, that his life on the road had lasted ages already, and that the events of the past month had been yet another age, did not know what to make of such a miscalculation. Was it possible that the man was right, and that in spite of his travel weariness and physical damage and deep feelings of sadness and loss, he was still not so old as all that? Though hesitant to take much hope from such a notion of his youthfulness—where could it possibly lead to, anyway?—Arthur was nonetheless pleased to note, as they drove between fields of rising corn, that for perhaps the first time in his travels, without either his own stories or the Professor's theories to fill the vacuum of time that engulfed the highway before them, someone had taken the trouble to look at him as an individual. And even though he knew that the look had not been entirely clear-sighted, he was pleased that it had at least been there. And so when the car stopped on the outskirts of Cincinnati to let him out, and the driver was leaning across the front seat to hand him his crutches, Arthur suddenly bent over and kissed him on the top of his shiny head, with gratitude.

# Chapter 13

WHEN ARTHUR arrived at the penitentiary he was treated
courteously but denied entrance. All visits had to be pre-
arranged, and the guards at the gate, in the cool late-morning
shadow of the stone wall where Arthur was not at all re-
luctant to pause for a while, after having had to walk the last
couple of miles to the prison, were adamant. But Arthur,
who had not come all this way merely to be turned away at
the gates, and who did not relish having to hobble out into
the summer sun again already, was equally persevering, until
at last the guards, taken by both his pathetic appearance and
the urgency of his pleas, arranged for him to see the warden.

In the warden's office, Arthur was offered a seat across a

steel desk from a man with thick gray hair and a kindly face. The guard who had accompanied Arthur from the gate remained standing behind his chair, and the warden fiddled with a sharp yellow pencil, sliding it back and forth between his thumb and index finger, while he explained gently that it was not possible for an inmate to have visitors on other than regular visiting days, that visits were only permitted by relatives or persons specially requested by the inmate, and that recently admitted inmates were automatically placed on probation for a period of several weeks, and therefore permitted no visitors during that time.

"But he's my father!" cried Arthur, "I have to see him!" The warden frowned at this outburst and rolled his chair around to the filing cabinet behind his desk. When he had found the folder he wanted, he turned back to face Arthur and opened it on his desk.

"It says here," he told Arthur very slowly, moving the eraser end of his pencil across the lines of a paper he had withdrawn from the folder, "that Mr. Melville is not and never has been married, and that he has no living relatives." He looked up at Arthur with a quizzical expression on his face.

"I mean he's been *like* a father to me," explained Arthur, "and besides, I don't have any other father. And I'm sure if he knew that I was here, he would make a special request to see me."

"Young man," said the warden with great patience, closing up the folder, slipping it back into the filing cabinet, and turning back to his pencil, "I'm sorry for you, but that's the way it is. You are neither son nor specially requested person. The inmate is not allowed to have visitors yet. Moreover, visiting day is not today but Sunday. This is Thursday. If you were going to be allowed to see him this coming Sunday, you would have had to have your application for a visit in by Wednesday. That was yesterday."

"All right," said Arthur, "I'll wait till next week."

"By the middle of next week," announced the warden, tapping his pencil on the desk, "Mr. Melville will have been transferred to the federal penitentiary in Walla Walla, Washington. Since that is where he is scheduled to serve the full term of his sentence, you will have plenty of time to visit him there." He opened a drawer in the center of his desk, dropped his pencil into it, and wished Arthur goodbye.

When the guard had escorted him back to the gate, and it had been opened to emit him into the outside world once more, and then shut quickly behind him, Arthur, finding that the wall which towered over him was now bathed with afternoon sunlight, and no longer afforded any shade, set out on foot and crutches toward the highway from which he had come. With luck, he thought, he might manage to be in Walla Walla by the time Professor Melville arrived there, or soon after. There he could wait, if necessary, until such time as visitation was permitted. In the meantime, he had never been that far west before, and it could be an interesting experience. There was nothing to prevent Stella from following him there; perhaps, being better informed than he, she was waiting there already. It was a place from which they might make a new beginning. And en route, he decided, as he arrived at last in sight of the road west, and spotted his first cripple edging onto the shoulder with the thum-thump of a flat tire, for it was a busy highway, he might well stop at the University just one more time. For there, after all, was the home of the Poughkeepsie Institute. And in what books and records of its existence yet remained in Dr. Wells' possession might yet be found the things he wanted to know, in order to understand how things had worked out as they had, concerning the Professor's plans, and what he himself might best do now. Perhaps, he concluded, cranking the jack to ease the car down onto the spare he had put on, he might even seek to reinvigorate the Poughkeepsie Institute, help it to flourish once again and, in so doing, both rescue Professor Melville from what promised to be almost a lifelong incarceration and, at the same time, set into motion once more the machinery which would work most effectively toward the dissemination of the Theory of Unteleology. The Institute was, he could not help thinking, his home, even his birthplace, in a manner of speaking, for it was there that the forces had arisen which jarred him loose from the decade-long rut he had worn along the East Coast, and turned him in new directions, and there, too, that Stella had first made her . . . what? miraculous? . . . appearance, and her remarkable discovery.

What he found when he got back there, however, with a long string of mechanical accomplishments, at which he was becoming increasingly adept, behind him, and an exceedingly agitated Dr. Wells, into whose office he had entered uninvited and unannounced, before him, was that there was no Poughkeepsie Institute, in reality.

"No, no, no!" cried Dr. Wells, scrambling around behind the cluttered desk in his paneled office and trying desperately to straighten up the papers he had knocked awry when Arthur entered. "There's no such thing as Poughkeepsie Institute. There never was. No place, no office, no nothing. Just Melville's name, unfortunately for him. The whole thing was only a legal fiction devised to channel funds for the completion of the *Cinderella*. Now it isn't even that.

There's nothing you can do with it. Now please go away, I'm expecting a client, there's no telling who saw you come in here!"

Arthur, taken quite aback by this wild outburst after the hopeful thoughts that had brought him here, and already backing toward the office door on unsteady crutches, could only mutter, "Nothing?"

"Wait, yes, there's something," snapped Wells, his hands darting around in the piles of papers on his desk until at last he came up with what he was searching for and came dashing out from behind his desk and across the room to Arthur with it, saying, "A letter from Melville, just arrived this morning, go on now, god bless you," and thrusting Arthur out and closing the door behind him.

Out on the street, Arthur found that a twenty-dollar bill had been thrust into his hand along with the letter. He stuffed the money into a pocket and tore the envelope, addressed to him care of Dr. Wells, open, but did not take the letter out until he had walked the dozen blocks back to the park near the university and found his old green bench unoccupied and sat down there and slid his crutches underneath the bench. Then, with a warm first of July sun beating down on his unkempt sandy hair, and children freed from school for the summer racing around the park's narrow pathways on foot and on scooters and tricycles, he extracted the letter and unfolded it and spread it out on his lap and began to read. "Dear Arthur," it began,

I am sorry I was not permitted to see you after the warden told me you came all that distance to visit me. He appears to be a nice man but is not really very ███████████. I guess I owe you several explanations and I would have preferred to make them in person, but I don't think they should wait until I get out of this place, since I am apparently going to be here for a good many years.

First of all, I was sorry to learn from Dr. Wells about your unfortunate landing and the loss of the ███████████, none of which, I hasten to assure you, was your fault, since the ████████ had been carefully programmed to come down in the ████████ ██████. I am at a total loss to explain why you ended up back in the swamps, but I can tell you why no one took note of your arrival. After the police had picked us up as soon as you left, and I had been hauled off to the ████████ County Jail to await arraignment, I read in the newspaper several days later that on the day of scheduled return, which I presume was also the day of your actual return, the entire East Coast radar network had been blacked out by a sudden power failure. Is it possible that this had any connection with our project? What with the loss of the ████████ and my own present ████████████ position, I suspect it is unlikely that we shall ever know for certain. I guess the best I can say, Arthur, is that things don't always work out for the best, but I guess, too, that we know why that is, don't we?

Maybe someday yet all of humanity will come to understand this, though it has proven impossible to broach the subject with anyone in this place, especially ████████████. As you no doubt know, the judge ruled all testimony on the ████████████ or on the ████████████████████ out of order in the courtroom and insisted on admitting only testimony on the financial question, as if that really had anything to do with it all.

At least that kept Stella out of the courtroom, though I suppose that by now you know better than I how she has fared, since the last time I saw her was in the county jail when she came to say good-bye. She showed me, before she left, the tracking device that she was still carrying in her purse, so I hope, for both of you, that has at least worked out all right, though I have had some doubts as to whether the batteries in your implant still have any life in them.

At any rate, please believe me when I say that I never intended harm to you or Stella or anyone else, but only hoped that we could all speed the day when the whole world might come to understand ███████████████. The fact that you found Stella and me in such a compromising ██████████ was, indeed, unfortunate, but the truth is that there was nothing between us. That unconsummated little scene was, I suppose, only the result of the tensions of the approaching climax of our project. It is, as she made clear to me on her final visit, only you Stella cares about. I am sure she will make you a fine wife.

I know this letter has already been much too long, but I want to say all I can say and then release you from any sense of obligation you may have to me. There is nothing I can do for you now, and I suppose we must assume that even ██████████████ will manage to get along all on its own, as it always has. May all go well with you, Arthur, or at least as well as might be expected, given our understanding of ███████████████.

Your Colleague,
Professor G. Melville

P.S. If, by any chance, you should still be possessed by the desire to discover more about your own nativity, let me remind you, in case you have forgotten, that your footprints are still on record in the hospital in your home town. Whatever you discover about your family, I am sure it will at least please you to have the definite facts in hand at last.

Yours again,
G.M.

All in all, Arthur found this a great deal to take in all at once, in the park. It was not so much what had been censored that left him unsettled, as what Professor Melville had not been able to say anything about at all. If he was relieved about what he learned of Stella, he was yet apprehensive with what he might yet find out about himself. If he had been released from something by the Professor, he had yet no idea of what it was he had been released to. And what of the Unteleology that, to Arthur's puzzlement, had nowhere in the letter managed to escape the censor's black pen? Was it such an unmentionable indeed? To be sure, it would get along on its own, under the terms of its own being. But what of the Professor's plans of putting the world at ease with it? What of humanity? What of himself, for that matter? How was Stella going to find him, if indeed the batteries in his homing device had gone dead, or he her, now that Dr. Wells had shut him out?

And where were the answers to all these questions? He was restless, suddenly, with the burden of their presence, and decided to get up and walk around a bit with them, now that the afternoon was waning and the air a little cooler, but when he reached for his crutches and started to stand up, a heavy hand fell on his shoulder from behind, and forced him down onto his bench again.

"There are these, too," said the voice from behind him. Arthur turned around and saw that it was Dr. Wells, carrying in his other arm a large, overstuffed manila envelope, which he dropped quickly onto Arthur's lap, as if it contained something unspeakably vile that he could not carry a step farther. Before Arthur could ask him what was in the envelope, he let loose a rapid torrent of words.

"Believe me," he said, speaking as rapidly as possible, "that's all there are, you'll remember I mentioned them before, take them, they're yours, there's nothing else, nothing, I have nothing else for you, there's nothing more I can do, please don't come near me any more, go away," but almost before he was finished speaking it was he who was going away, scurrying quickly down the walk and out of the park, while Arthur, turning back now to see what lay in his lap that might have caused Dr. Wells such consternation, accidentally knocked the manila envelope to the ground beside his crutches, and saw hundreds of elaborately printed stock certificates come spilling forth from it, each engraved with the name of the Poughkeepsie Institute, in large gothic letters, and bearing in one corner its gold seal, emblazoned with a question mark.

# Chapter 14

O N  T H E  following day Arthur set out in an old brown Pontiac in search of his nativity. It was clear enough, from the letter, that there was no point in following Professor Melville west; the Professor neither wanted him to do so nor had any further information or advice to give him. It was equally clear that he could expect no further help from Dr. Wells, or from the long-gone Dr. Kent, who had flown to the safety of distance, and that there was, therefore, nothing to be gained by hanging around the University any longer. Stella was neither likely to look for him there nor, given the sorry state of his batteries, to be drawn to him there. What he had figured out, on the early-morning city bus that he had taken in order to get most quickly to the outskirts of town, and the highway east, was that on his way to visit the hospital, where his infant footprints were recorded, he might well stop in to talk with old Mr. Hoppe, on the slight chance that he might there pick up some clue as to where Stella might have gone in an emergency, or to whom.

Under his shirt, safely buttoned up next to his skin, Arthur had the envelope full of stock certificates, with the exception of one which had gone sailing off in the light summer breeze while he was gathering up the others that had spilled to the ground beside his park bench. A little boy had chased it and finally caught it at the base of an elm tree, but before he could make off with it his mother had grabbed him by the arm and marched him straight back to Arthur, to return his prize. Arthur had explained to her that it was nothing of value, and that the boy was welcome to keep it. She looked dubious, but finally gave in when Arthur showed her he had hundreds of others just like it. Arthur watched the woman as she left the park, then, and saw her grab the certificate from her son's hand, peer closely at it, return it to him, walk on, grab it again, examine it, return it, and so on, over and over again, till they turned the corner at the end of the block, and were lost to his sight.

Arthur also had grease-blackened fingers from cleaning the plugs and points of the Pontiac for its elderly driver. The car was in remarkably fine condition for its age, especially considering the fact that, as Arthur had seen with his now-expert eye, no care whatsoever had been given to its engine. Once Arthur had it humming again, and they were out on the highway, the old man drove the car extremely fast, as if he were long accustomed to treating the posted maximum speed limits as minimums. He had neatly barbered gray hair, wild, untrimmed, bushy gray mustaches, wore a brown suit with vest that almost exactly matched the color of his car, and told Arthur that he was on his way to play in a senior citizens' golf tournament at a hot-springs resort in southern Indiana. There was, in fact, a very new-looking golf bag, filled with shiny clubs, lying on the back seat, side by side with Arthur's crutches.

Arthur was not at all used to sticking with single rides for such great distances. In the old days, in fact, he would, if he had thought of it, have considered it almost beneath his dignity, especially in such an ancient vehicle as this. He had accepted his rides, almost casually for the most part, had told his stories, and then frequently grown impatient, for a new story, or a change of car or company, or just inexplicably impatient, and often asked to be let out, even though that same driver was headed straight on down the road toward Arthur's own destination. None of it had much seemed to matter; things had always worked out pretty much all right, and he had always, until the last time, got to where he was going to. Now, however, he was anxious, he was not at all sure that things were going to work out all right, any longer, and he was exceedingly pleased that the old man was going to move him at such high speed to a point not too far from his destination, that small town in northwestern Ohio where he had been born, and where, before going off to the University, he had been raised within the warm glow of family and financial security provided by Arthur Hoppe, Jr., whom he had formerly believed to be his father.

There was something of the same warm, comfortable aura in the gentleman who now drove Arthur eastward at such breakneck speed, over rich, rolling fields where the corn already stood shoulder high, and around cities that were blurred in dense, smoggy summer haze. They drove all day and on through the night, without stopping except for brief spells at gas stations and roadside diners, and the old man showed no sign at all of tiring, though Arthur often dozed for several hours at a time. The old fellow talked incessantly, too, about his far-flung, prosperous, happy family, about his golf games with corporate board chairmen and college presidents, and finally, far along into the night, when Arthur had had so much sleep he could not help but listen, about his own financial investments, and his great worries about them.

"Listen, son," he said, nudging Arthur to make sure he was still awake, "you think it's all gravy owning stocks and bonds. Thought so myself when I was your age. Just clip, deposit, and spend, or wait for the checks to come rolling in. Well, I can tell you it's not like that at all. Fact is, it's nothing but worry, worry, worry. Rough on the heart, hard on the family, and hell on the golf game. And that's just the added worry, not the real worry, about the stocks themselves."

"Why is that, sir?" asked Arthur.

"It's the market," the old man told him, "supply and demand, fluctuating economic forces, war and peace, tight money, research and development, public confidence, the government. You just never know. It's nothing but worry, worry, worry." The sky was beginning to grow lighter out above the horizon in front of them.

"How would you like," said Arthur, sitting up very thoughtfully, "to own a stock you didn't have to worry about?"

"I tell you," said the old man, "it's all worry and nothing but. Even now I ought to be trying to figure out what's the matter with my chip shot, that I'm not getting enough loft, but what am I doing? Worrying about my stocks, that's what." He bore down noticeably harder on the accelerator. Arthur sat up straighter still. The sky was rapidly becoming brighter and brighter.

"Look," said Arthur. He unbuttoned the top buttons of

his shirt and withdrew the manila envelope from its place of safety and pulled one of the stock certificates out of the envelope.

"May I borrow a pen, please?" said Arthur. The old man plucked a solid-gold fountain pen from his inside jacket pocket and handed it over to Arthur.

"What's your name, sir?" asked Arthur. The old man told him and Arthur carefully printed it in on the line marked "Bearer." Then he returned the pen and, when the old man had put it away, passed him the stock certificate as well.

"Look," said Arthur again. The sun was just clearing the horizon dead ahead of them.

"By god," said the old man, "it's a real stock certificate, that's for sure. Properly signed and sealed and everything. Even spells my name right. Only you've forgot to fill in here where it says "Number of Shares." He passed the stock certificate back to Arthur, and his pen with it. Where it said "Number of Shares" Arthur wrote "One (1)" and returned it to him.

"That's right," said the old man, "and is it recorded in the stock transfer book too?"

"That's here too," said Arthur. He pulled the thin ledger out of the envelope and dutifully registered the first share of stock in the old man's name and penned his own initials beside it. Then he made sure everything was put away in its proper place again: the pen, the registry ledger, and, finally, the manila envelope. When he was done, it was broad daylight, in Indiana.

"Well," said the old man, trying to adjust the visor to keep the morning sun out of his eyes, "I suppose you know what you've done now?"

"What's that, sir?" asked Arthur.

"Given me something else to worry about, that's what."

"No, sir," said Arthur, "that's the whole point. I've given you a share of stock in what I honestly believe to be one of our most vital organizations, the Poughkeepsie Institute. It is totally involved with the health and welfare of this country and the world, and yet it has no plant or payroll, turns out no products, produces neither profit nor loss, and its stock is utterly valueless. Nothing to worry about, see?"

"Defunct, huh?" said the old man. "Bankrupt?"

"No, sir," said Arthur, rolling his window part way down now that the day was beginning to warm up, "not defunct, not so long as I'm still around. Just not going anywhere." They stopped for breakfast then, and the old man folded up his share of stock in the Poughkeepsie Institute and tucked it thoughtfully away in his coat pocket. After breakfast they drove on in silence for several more hours, until they arrived at the turn-off for the resort, and the old man pulled to the side of the road to let Arthur out of the car.

"But there's always hope, isn't there?" he said, handing Arthur his crutches, "Always a chance?"

"No, sir," said Arthur, "none at all."

"Oh," said the old man, closing the door. "Well, I guess that does make a difference, doesn't it?"

"Then you won't worry about it?" said Arthur, poking his head in through the half-open window.

"No," said the old man, "I guess I won't. I guess I'll think about my chip shot for a while."

# Chapter 15

B Y T H E following morning at eight o'clock, leaning wearily on his crutches by the side of the road at the top of the rise that overlooked his home town from the southwest, Arthur had given away thirty-two single shares of stock in the Pough-keepsie Institute. He had given one to each person he had ridden with, and it had taken him quite a few rides to cover this last stretch of his journey. He had given several to waitresses and even more to customers in the half-dozen roadside diners he and his drivers had stopped at. He had tried carefully not to be pushy, because some people, he found, were almost automatically suspicious, and refused to accept the certificates, and though Arthur didn't see how the certificates could do them any harm—after all, he thought, if they

wanted, they could even throw them away as soon as he left
—still he didn't want anybody to feel bad about them. That
wasn't their purpose, as he saw it. If they had a purpose,
which Arthur really doubted, it was only to be something
that no one had to worry about, something that everyone
could be at ease with, whether he had millions invested in
the stock market or whether he had never even seen a share
of stock before. He gave away three to gas-station attendants
and one to a state patrol officer who stopped them on the
highway in the middle of the night and issued the driver a
warning ticket for faulty rear lights. Arthur dutifully waited
till the policeman had finished writing out the ticket before
he gave him the certificate, so that there would be no suspicion of attempted bribery. Once on the previous afternoon
he and the middle-aged woman in whose convertible he was
riding, after he had found her parked along the highway with
her top half up and half down and had persuaded it to go all
the way down and stay there, decided to give away certificates to the next five people they saw walking beside the
road. They had to stop thirteen times before they finally
found five who would take them, and three of those were
children. All of these Arthur painstakingly recorded, by
name and number, in the stock registry ledger.

The thirty-second share went to the young farmer in the
gray double-breasted suit who drove Arthur the last eighty
miles, in his gleaming blue Cadillac, and deposited him on
the rise overlooking town. Arthur had found him swearing
over a flat tire just about at dawn, and had changed it for
him so the young man wouldn't ruin his suit. But when the
tire had been changed and they were on their way, he showed
Arthur a long tear in one of his pants legs.

"Damn barbed wire!" he said. He told Arthur how he
drove way over into Indiana three or four nights a week to

visit his fiancée. She lived all alone with her widowed father, who didn't think it was time for her to get married yet, Cadillac or no, so he had to come over way past midnight, when the old man was sound asleep, and sneak across most of their big farm and quiet the dogs and get in through the back window because the doors were always bolted up tight and then get out in time in the morning, before the old man was up for chores. And now the old man had taken to laying strands of barbed wire here and there around the place of late, and he'd caught one with his leg this morning and another with the car and was fit to be tied, because it was just too much, all this running around, and here he was ruining his good clothes and maybe getting his new car all scratched up, and just not fit to do a proper day's work on his own farm any more, the way things were going.

Arthur, hoping he could perhaps help the young man calm down and make him feel a little better, took out a stock certificate and offered it to him, but he just pushed it away.

"Shit," he told Arthur, "I've got stocks silo high. Got mutual funds, treasury notes, and tax-free municipal bonds. Got an account in every bank in the county and property in Florida and Arizona. Got four hundred prize hogs and the best sixteen pieces of farm equipment you ever seen, and don't owe a penny on it. What'd I need your lousy share of stock for?"

"Nothing," said Arthur, who was disappointed that he had only managed to make the young farmer more excited and was more than willing to put the certificate away and forget about it. "Nothing, I guess."

"Here," said his companion, "let me see that," and he grabbed the certificate back out of Arthur's hands and spread it out across the steering wheel to look at it as he drove.

"Poughkeepsie Institute," he said, "what's this? I've got

G.E. and A.T.&T. and T.W.A. and P.C.G.&E. I got stocks I know and stocks that'll go with the market. But what's this? Where's this going?" He pounded at the certificate with one hand, and the Cadillac's horn blared at the empty highway.

"Nowhere," answered Arthur. But the young farmer still held on to the certificate as they roared along into Ohio and, in the end, decided to keep it. He seemed greatly calmed as Arthur affixed his name both to the certificate and the registry. And when he stopped on the rise west of town to let Arthur out, before he turned off on the county road toward his farm, he patted Arthur wearily on the arm as he said goodbye and pointed sheepishly at the gaping tear in his pants.

"Aw, shit," he said as Arthur climbed out of the car, "it's just a lousy suit."

From the top of the rise, standing beside the little sign that read "Population 5,023" and had read just the same when he was a boy growing up in the town, and no one had known even then whether or not that was an accurate figure, he could see all the way across to the small rise on the east side of the town, where the hospital stood. That was pretty much the way he remembered the town: with the hospital on the hill to the east and the County Home on the hill to the west, and the main street running from one to the other, crossed itself by a number of lesser streets and, as one went out of town to the east, by a small stream, which one crossed on a stone bridge, and then by the railroad tracks, at a level crossing. Except that the hills weren't so high as he remembered and the old folks' home was no longer standing on the western rise. He remembered that it had burned down just before he went off to college, and that when the townspeople realized that the inmates weren't lunatics but merely old people, from all over the county, who might enjoy being able to toddle into town every once in a while, they allowed it to be rebuilt at the foot of the slope, just on the edges of the Main Street business district. It was toward this yellow brick structure that Arthur now hobbled downhill, noting beyond it, as he went, an unusual amount of activity in the town for that hour of the morning.

In the small, tiled lobby of the County Home for the Aged and Infirm Arthur received appropriate directions from the receptionist, followed the long gleaming hallway of the east wing almost to its very end, found the proper room number posted above the doorway, hopped aside to allow a muscular, heavily tanned man, whose handsome features were set off both by hair silvering at the temples and the rugged bush jacket he wore, to exit, and, entering the room himself, found old Mr. Hoppe sitting in a straight-backed chair in the warm sunlight that flowed through the window of his room. He looked terribly aged and small—Arthur remembered him as always having been very old, but also as having been a man of sizable stature—but he looked up at Arthur with a broad smile on his narrow face, so that Arthur himself could not help smiling with pleasure when he saw how glad the old man, whom he had not even expected to recognize him, was to see him.

"Well," said Arthur Hoppe, Jr., beaming, "well, well, well. What d'ya think?"

"I'm pleased to see you, sir," said Arthur. He started to sit down on the edge of the bed, but stopped, realizing he was probably too dirty to do that. There was, however, no other chair in the room, so he had no choice but to stand uncomfortably in its center, facing the chair where the old man sat.

"What's that?" said the old man, leaning forward.

"It's good to be home, sir," said Arthur, realizing, however, that this was not home at all, for either of them, and that might not have been the best thing to say.

"Home?" said Mr. Hoppe.

"Yes, sir," said Arthur, who supposed he would have to stick with what he had committed himself to.

"Who're you?" said Mr. Hoppe.

"It's me," said Arthur, "Arthur." It was he who leaned forward now, to make sure the old man could see him.

"Oh," said Mr. Hoppe, "it's you. Where've you been? What did you think of him?"

"Of who?"

"My son."

"No, sir," said Arthur, "I know now that I'm not really your son, but it doesn't really make any difference. I'm grateful for all that you did for me. I . . . ."

"I guess you're just back to make sure you get included in my will," snapped the old man.

"No, sir," said Arthur, "I just want to ask about Stella."

"What's that?" said Mr. Hoppe. He suddenly got a very crafty look on his face and slid downward in his chair. "That's nothing, that's what. You don't know what you're talking about."

"I just thought you might have some information," Arthur began.

"All right, then," the old man interrupted, snapping straight back up in his chair, "I'll put you in the will. Always meant to anyway. Snippy letter, my boy, snippy letter. I suppose you thought I'd forgotten that, old fool that I am. But I'll put you in all the same. You're a good boy at heart, always were. Consider it done. That satisfy you?"

"No, sir," said Arthur, who could not see how being in the Hoppe will was any solution to his quest for Stella, "I mean, I'm grateful, but that's not what I came for at all."

"Well," snapped Mr. Hoppe, "if you came to see my son, you're too late. He's off again faster than you can say 'Jack Robinson.' You just missed him, but fact is, he never did settle down in any one place long enough to get the chair warm. Been that way ever since he was a tike."

Arthur had nothing at all to say to this, for he suddenly realized that the handsome, middle-aged, athletic-looking man who had swaggered out of the room just as he was about to enter must have been none other than the Hoppes' true son, Jack, who was supposed to have been killed in a plane crash prior to his own adoption but of whom he had never heard a word from Mr. Hoppe himself.

"Old Jack," chuckled Mr. Hoppe, rocking forward and back in his chair.

"That gentleman?" said Arthur quietly, still dazed, half-gesturing at the doorway.

"Gentleman, my foot," answered Mr. Hoppe, still chuckling. "Just you ask any of the girls around here! There's some fathers was happier than they'd care to admit when the news come back of him being down in the jungle. Just as well he didn't show his face around town when he came back that first time. Been just about everywhere since then too. Himalayas, Antarctica, Africa, South Pacific, Amazon jungles two or three times since. Oh, he always was the wild one, him. Off to China now. Says he don't expect he'll make it back from this one. How about that! I guess he's well on the way already." The old man turned and looked out the window, as if he might catch a glimpse of Jack's plane rising and banking and turning toward China, and dipping its wings in farewell.

"I guess that's fine," said Arthur, who didn't know what else to say, but felt he ought to say something all the same.

"Oh," said Mr. Hoppe without turning around, "you're a

fine boy too, Arthur. I have high hopes for you. Just no family secrets now, you hear? I'll write you a fine letter of recommendation, that's what. Then you'll really go places. Oh, that old Jack, doesn't he go, though!"

While the old man continued talking excitedly to the window about Jack, Arthur slipped out of the room, pausing, as he left, to make out a stock certificate and leave it on Mr. Hoppe's bed. He gave another to an old crone sitting in a wheel chair in the hallway, and stopped in the lobby to give another one to the white-uniformed receptionist. There was a great deal of noise coming from the outside, and many of the old people were gathered by the front door. The receptionist told Arthur she had never seen a share of stock, and squealed like a much younger woman than she really was when Arthur wrote out her name on it and in the registry book.

"Ooooooh," she said, "will I get rich?"

"No," Arthur assured her, "you won't get rich."

"Well," she smiled, "thanks for telling me, anyway. I guess I always knew I'd never get rich." Arthur asked her about the noise and the gathering at the doorway.

"It's the Fourth of July," she told him.

When Arthur stepped out into the street, he found that it truly was the Fourth of July. There was a band from the Consolidated High School lining up right in front of the County Home. Two drum majorettes were limbering up their twirling arms in front of the band, and the Boy Scouts and the American Legion and the Ladies' Auxiliary and the Little League baseball team, plus the usual collection of unorganized children, were all finding their places behind them. Arthur, who had no desire to remain in the town longer than was absolutely necessary, was anxious to get right to the hospital. He knew that if he didn't hurry the parade would soon be under way, packing the street so full of marchers and on-lookers that it would take him all morning to make his way across town. So he hobbled as quickly as he could out into the bright mid-morning sun and was well on his way by the time he heard the band strike up its first marching tune. He stopped in the middle of town, in front of the Woolworth's store, to see how far ahead he was, and when he saw that he had a good lead on them he stood there for a while to catch his breath and cool off. Then when they were about a block off, and stepping ahead in high style, with the majorettes prancing out in front of them, and the crowd starting to flow down toward where he stood, he started off again. He looked back over his shoulder at the drugstore and again as he passed the liquor store, and found that they were gaining steadily on him, and when he was crossing the bridge over the little stream that ran through town he looked back again, because the noise of the band was so loud it sounded like they were right on top of him, and found they were less than half a block away, so he put on a final burst of speed, seeing the hospital up on the rise right ahead of him now, and then looked back just once more as he was crossing the railroad tracks, but before he could see where the band was, his right crutch caught in the first rail and spilled him to the ground, across the tracks, and he was just in the middle of pulling himself off the tracks, and was sitting up surprised to see that the band had fallen silent and had come to a halt in the middle of the bridge, where the majorettes stood staring open-mouthed with their batons lying in the dust in front of them, when the only train of the day came rolling through and sliced his remaining leg neatly off just below the knee.

# Chapter 16

THE FIRST thing that Arthur said when he woke up in the hospital later that same day was, "Where is my leg?" When no one answered him and he looked around, in some pain, to see that, in fact, no one was there, he reached for the buzzer to call the nurse, but apparently he had expressed himself loudly enough the first time, because before he could ring she came scurrying into his room urging him to be quiet, very quiet, and gently forcing his head back down upon the pillow. While he tried haltingly to explain to her that it was a practical, not a hysterical, question that he was attempting to ask her, she calmly injected into his vein a fine soporific fluid that left him suspended in mid-sentence. When he awoke in the middle of the night and hollered out the same question as loudly as he could, in hopes that someone within hearing distance would enter with the answer, he received the same treatment. And when he woke the next time, with the sunlight streaming through his window, he saw that the nurse was already there, standing beside his bed, asking how he felt this morning. He started to ask the same question as before, choked it back before he had let any of the words loose, looked over at the nurse, saw that this time she did not have a syringe in her hand, and then went ahead and asked it.

She ignored him at first, and when he realized that she might not be the same nurse as the night before, he repeated his question again, but she went on silently with her business of tidying up the room and bringing his breakfast tray over to him. She was a tall, elderly woman, and with her hair tied back in a bun behind her cap, she had a lean, efficient look about her which suggested to Arthur a certain lack of sympathy. But he was determined and kept on asking his question, in a voice that grew louder and louder, until at last she turned about to face him and informed him in no uncertain terms that what he was asking was not a proper question at all.

"People just don't ask questions like that," she concluded. "It's not a proper matter for discussion."

Arthur, ignoring his breakfast, by no means able to ignore the pain that still coursed sharply upward from the point of amputation, tried to explain to her how it was, indeed, not only a proper but a necessary matter for discussion. Speaking very slowly, he told her how he had traveled a great distance on account of that leg, because it was here that he had been born, here that his infant footprints had been recorded for identification purposes, and therefore here, at this very hospital, at which he had arrived in so unexpected a fashion, after coming so close to getting there on his own terms, that he might, by comparing the footprint from his recently lost leg, wherever it now was, be able to discover his true paternity.

"Oh, yes," the nurse assured him, "we have records like that of every baby ever born here. I used to take those little footprints myself, all those years when I worked in OB, but that was a long, long time ago." She sat down across from Arthur on the unoccupied second bed in the room, next to the little nightstand on which, Arthur saw, lay his manila folder containing the stock certificates. "I bet," she went on, "I've worked in every section of this hospital, oh, this used to be a real busy place, served four counties back then. Now every town has its own little clinic and everybody who's anybody goes off to Toledo when they really need a hospital." Then she fell silent and sat there near Arthur with a sad, faraway look in her eyes.

"My leg," Arthur gently reminded her, through his own pain.

"Oh," she said, looking very startled.

"No leg," Arthur added, "no father."

"You poor boy." She suddenly looked very sad and thoughtful again. "Not ever to have known a father."

Arthur assured her that he had indeed known a father, a very kindly one too, who had been an exceedingly good father to him, though he himself had perhaps not always been as good a son as he ought to have been, but that that was not his *real* father, and now he wanted to know who his real father was and what he needed to find that out was his leg, which he no longer had, not either of them now. Where was his leg? What had they done with his leg?

She supposed that they had done the usual thing with it. She also supposed, with a kind of weary sadness, that she could go and check on it, if that was what the patient really wanted. He did. Finally, however, halfway to the door, she turned around and supposed that if Arthur really was who he was supposed to be, it was not necessary to have the leg after all, to know who he was.

"Why is that?" asked Arthur.

"I have seen your birth certificate," said the nurse.

"How's that?" said Arthur.

"I filled it out myself," she told him. She came back and sat heavily down on the edge of the other bed again. "I worked almost ten years in delivery. Washed babies, took their footprints, put drops in their eyes, filled out birth certificates. Whole generation around here I helped bring into the world, though maybe most has gone away by now, like you." She paused and closed her eyes.

"And you're sure you filled out *my* birth certificate?" asked Arthur.

"Didn't make no difference," she said, looking up at him. "Old banker Hoppe was the richest man in town. Anything happened to him or his, everybody knew about it, fast as that." She snapped her fingers in Arthur's face. Arthur winced and said that he, for one, didn't know anything about it. She supposed he didn't, or he wouldn't have been there. She'd been fit to be tied yesterday when they brought him in, and said who they thought he was, because of whom he had been seen visiting at the Old Home. She had sent one of the off-duty orderlies over to the Home to question the old man on whether or not it really was Arthur, but instead the orderly had tried to explain what had happened, and Mr. Hoppe suddenly became suspicious that the hospital, which had come every year to try to get him to endow a new wing, or a new operating room, was after him for money again, and denied everything, saying, "My son's in China," and then becoming very confused and muttering, "He can't be dead yet, he only left this morning." This last she and the rest of the staff took as firm evidence that the old man had, indeed, just seen his son Arthur again.

"I saw him," said Arthur, "but he's not my father."

"I suppose not!" said the nurse.

"But you were there when I was born!" cried Arthur. "You filled out my birth certificate. You said so yourself. Who did it say my father was?"

"It didn't," she said, very quietly.

"What do you mean, '*it didn't*'?" screamed Arthur. "Everyone has a father! I must have had one too! I suppose it didn't say who my mother was either!"

"No," said the nurse, "it didn't say who your mother was either, but she was right there all the time. She was old banker Hoppe's niece, his dear dead sister's daughter, Maryjane, whose father was killed in the war. I went to high school with her."

"His niece!" cried Arthur.

"He did what he could for her," said the nurse, "even to keeping her name off the birth certificate, which only a man of his influence could do. I think that was when the new lobby was added. And of course he took you as his own child, to quiet the scandal down, what with his own son dead and gone, but old Mrs. Hoppe, she never got over the things that was said . . ."

"What did they say?" asked Arthur.

". . . and that poor child," continued the nurse, "was just doomed, I tell you. No one could ever control her, not even old Hoppe, when he took her into his house. She was a wild one, she was. Just like his own son. Wild ones all in that family, even some stories about the old man in his younger days. I tell you," she added, and fell silent.

"Tell me what?" asked Arthur.

What she told him, in a solemn, authoritative voice, was

that only a little more than two years later the old man had once again brought to the hospital an exceedingly pregnant Maryjane, demands for the same secrecy as before, and, this time, a check for the new ambulance. Only on this occasion all had not gone as well, for the mother had died in child-birth and Mr. Hoppe, deserted now by both his wife and niece, and already burdened with the care of one infant, was not willing to take the newborn girl to his bosom as well.

"Stella!" cried Arthur.

"I think that was what they called her," said the nurse. "They say he sent her off to a foster home and kind of looked after her all the time, and I guess no one ever blamed him for that, but . . ."

"Then," interrupted Arthur mournfully, suddenly feeling a great burst of pain explode from his leg, as if the accident had just this moment happened, "she *is* my sister after all, or at least my half-sister."

"At least," said the nurse.

"And everybody's known this," said Arthur, "but me."

"Lots of talk in a small town," said the nurse.

"And I didn't need to come here and lose my leg," said Arthur, "because it wouldn't have done me any good even if I'd kept it."

"No, it wouldn't," said the nurse.

"Because the whole town knew all about me anyway."

"More or less," said the nurse, "at least we heard you was doing real well in college, and then we didn't hear no more."

"Then," said Arthur, "you must also know who my father was!"

"I think," said the nurse, getting up and crossing the room, "it's time for your shot."

"Who was he?" demanded Arthur, reaching out to grab her as she went past him, but missing, and feeling the pain flare up in his leg again. The nurse paused at the foot of his bed and looked across at him.

"Most everybody says," she said, "it was his son." When Arthur, sinking down into his pain, failed to respond to this, she went on, saying, "Some says his son wasn't killed in the plane crash, neither, but came back a couple years later and was the father of the second child, too. And then," she added, "some says worse things than that, but I wouldn't pay no attention to such talk, if I was you."

"Ohhh," moaned Arthur, the pain welling up all around him now. "Why am I here? Why am I here?"

"To get well," said the nurse, approaching him again, with a syringe in her hands.

"How long?" he muttered.

"A few weeks," she said, wiping a spot on his arm with an alcohol pad.

"And then what?" he moaned softly. "I can't even walk at all any more."

"And then," she said, sliding the needle in under his skin, "we'll fit you with a nice set of artificial limbs, so you *can* walk. Or we'll give you a little wooden platform, with wheels. It's your choice."

"I think," said Arthur, in a barely audible voice, as both pain and consciousness slid from him, "I'll ride."

# Chapter 17

WHEN HE was released from the hospital in early August, Arthur had a new pair of pants, neatly pinned up at the knees; a brand new rubber-wheeled wooden platform with a padded seat and a pair of leather knuckle guards, to keep him from getting his hands all scraped up when he rolled himself along; a few dollars left over from what Dr. Wells had given him, so long ago; and the worn manila envelope containing the Poughkeepsie Institute stock certificates and Stock Transfer Ledger, minus, of course, those certificates he had given to the nurses, doctors, and orderlies who had attended to him there. He did not have any idea where he was going. He only knew that wherever it was, it had best be where Stella could never find him, now that he had found out that she was his half-sister, at least.

But as he paused on the concrete walk in front of the hospital, at the very summit of the small rise which overlooked the town on the west, and, on the east, broad fields, stretching down and out from the very top of the hill, where the tall corn was already tasseled out, an idea of direction at last occurred to him that seemed, lacking any other, as good as any he was liable to come up with. Professor Melville, he reasoned, had gone as far as he could, with Unteleology and the Poughkeepsie Institute, before being immobilized, more or less permanently, by circumstances. Might not he, Arthur, do much the same thing, and in so doing carry the Professor's work as far forward as he was able? He would head west, then, in the same direction that Professor Melville had last gone. Perhaps he would get just as far. Perhaps not. Perhaps farther. But he would go along as best he could, in his usual hitchhiking fashion, giving away, or attempting to give away, to each person he encountered, a share of stock in the Poughkeepsie Institute, which, as he had carefully informed all to whom he had given such certificates so far, was "not going anywhere." And when the certificates had been all given away, then he, too, would not go anywhere, any more, but would simply settle down right there, as soon as he had given away the last certificate, wherever that was, permanently, more or less. And of necessity, forever Stella-less.

With this plan in mind, Arthur wheeled himself rapidly across the road to where he might pick up the westbound traffic. The manila envelope lay snugly wedged between his legs as he waited there, in the hot midsummer sun, for his first ride. But noontime came and went, and many a car rolled by and dipped downhill toward the center of town without so much as pausing, and the hot sun beat upon him, and, from time to time, a face he recognized paused at a window of the hospital, to look across at him. He had left his crutches behind at the hospital, he realized, for a sort of vehicle of his own, which he had not thought at first a bad idea, but now he also became aware that he had left behind his visibility. For if, before, motorists had seen him standing there, and chosen to pass him by, what chance for a ride did he have now, when he rested almost at ground level, and there was little chance of his even being noticed from a passing car?

But just then, casting around for some sort of leafy branch, perhaps, which he thought to wave to attract attention, Arthur saw that a car coming uphill toward him, from the east, was faltering on the slope, came, steaming, to a halt, paused, and then rolled slowly back down several yards and off to the side of the road. Arthur, turning his little cart about, rolled quickly downhill toward it, where he found an elderly couple with three very tiny children, all wringing their hands in despair, for they had hoped to be home in time for supper. Arthur soothed them with his sense of mechanical competency, a touch he was pleased to find he had not forgotten. They rested while the car cooled down, then they fetched water from a nearby farm, while Arthur tinkered with their thermostat, which the old man first removed and then replaced at his instructions, until at last the car was ready to go again, and, with Arthur now in their midst, and his cart stuck out of the way in the trunk, they climbed the rest of the hill brightly and easily, descended into the town, rolled quickly through it and up and over the hill on the other side, and so carried Arthur westward, children and old people chattering birdlike all about him as he inscribed shares of stock for each of them, describing, as he did so, their utter lack of value.

Perhaps, Arthur thought, as ride after ride carried him farther west, in anything but a straight line, he might, as he went, find something, somewhere, in the way of sign that would indicate to him what he ought best to do, or whether the plan he had already devised was . . . appropriate, was the only word that occurred to him. Nothing of note happened to him, however, from which he could derive any implications of approval or disapproval, or any alternative paths of action. It was only the process of hitchhiking itself that underwent subtle changes, whose significance, if any, he was at a loss to determine. The fact that, seated on his cart, he could hardly be seen by most drivers left him more than ever at the mercy of mechanical cripples. These, on the other hand, appeared to Arthur to become more frequent than ever before, though it also seemed to him that the farther west he went, the shorter distance each ride carried him. The nature of the mechanical breakdowns also seemed to him to be getting increasingly complex, though he was equally pleased to find that, no doubt due to all the experience he was gaining, his own skills grew, on each occasion, to meet the problems at hand. Rarely did he come across a flat tire any more, nor was he, in his present condition, best suited for such work. Now he tore down carburetors, rewired electrical systems, coaxed balky fuel pumps into action. He had, because of his last unfortunate accident, a difficult time meeting the physical demands of his work, but he soon learned to lie back on his cart and slide under the front end of the car or, when necessary, to ask its occupants to lift him up onto one of the front fenders, and to assist him with the removal and replacement of parts.

He was also aided in this need for physical assistance by the fact that on this present journey he seemed to obtain rides only in cars which were occupied by groups of people, whereas in the past he had hardly ever been given a ride unless there was only the driver in the car. No longer did he seem to find solitaries abandoned by the side of the road, trying to puzzle out what was wrong with their cars. Now it was always two or three, at least, and often four or five, and sometimes even more, whom he found standing around the upraised hood. He was at a total loss to explain this phenomenon, and soon gave up any attempt to do so, as the days and the miles crept slowly by. He was satisfied so long as his generally westerly direction was maintained, as it was in a curious zigzagging way that often took so many turns in a southerly or northerly direction that he was a good many days in crossing a state from east to west. Having neither a set destination nor a schedule of any sort, he was not frustrated, either, by the fact that some of his repairs were often a day or more in the making, especially when a driver or passenger had to be dispatched to the nearest town to find a needed part. He was, in a way, pleased, not only by the amount of company he now found but by the fact that, encountering such sizable groups as he now did, his supply of stock certificates was rapidly dwindling. The manila envelope grew tattered and thin; Indiana, Illinois, Wisconsin, corners even of Michigan and Iowa, fell gradually behind him as August edged into September; the end of his journey, Arthur knew, was clearly in sight.

Most of those groups which carried him westward thus, to his unknown destination, were, of course, families, frequently on their way to or from summer vacations, their cars loaded not only with children but with games, toys, souvenirs, pets, and picnic lunches, so that Arthur frequently found himself squeezed into incredible corners, invited to play chess or cribbage or count-the-cows, enlisted to settle sibling rivalries or dispose of soiled diapers, and fed a relatively unchanging diet of bologna and cheese sandwiches, potato chips, pickles, and cookies. To each member of each such family that he rode with, adults and children and infants alike, and often an elderly aunt or grandmother as well, Arthur gave a share of stock in the Poughkeepsie Institute, carefully inscribing the individual's name on the certificate and in his registry, and explaining, as he did so, the nature of his gift: that it was worthless stock, that the Institute was not and never would be going anywhere, that this share of stock, therefore, laid upon the recipient no burden of obligation or worry, nothing but whatever joy he might get just from having it, for what it was, which was not much.

Thus did Arthur spread the last remaining certificates far and wide across the Midwest: to a group of five brothers from Indiana, all butchers, making their way slowly from cousin to cousin toward a convention in Kansas City; to a group of third-grade teachers from Wisconsin who were returning from a trip to Mammoth Cave; to a group of tall socialist poets who were trying to locate forty acres of woodland which one of them, who had had a brief career with the Detroit Tigers, had purchased in western Illinois; to groups of college kids wending slowly toward the huge state universities of Minnesota and Nebraska and Oklahoma; to dancers and siding salesmen and horse trainers and revenue agents and the members of a traveling professional bridge tournament who were trying to decide whether or not to fulfill their engagement in Bismarck. Far and away his favorite group was a carload of jazz musicians from Toronto whose great shouts of glee roared through the open car windows and out over the Iowa cornfields and into the night when Arthur presented them with their stock certificates, because, as they told him, if there was one thing for damn sure, it was that they weren't going anywhere either.

But the last share of stock in the Poughkeepsie Institute went to the sole solitary individual with whom Arthur rode on this journey, a shaggy-bearded, long-haired young man with fine, white, long fingers whom Arthur had found tinkering with an ancient pickup truck beside a road on the empty plains of western Minnesota. When they had gotten the gas line cleaned out and flowing again, the young man drove Arthur on west a way, sticking mainly to the county roads and the older state highways because, he explained, it was Labor Day, and the main thoroughfares were too crowded and dangerous. As they drove through the hot September afternoon, the young man talked quietly about what nice country it was there, while Arthur carefully withdrew the last share, asked the young man his name, inscribed it on both stock and book, handed the certificate to him, tucked the register under his shirt, and crumpled the old manila envelope into a ball and tossed it out the window. They were climbing a gentle slope above the Minnesota River valley, and when they got to the top the young man stopped the truck. Then he got out and came around to Arthur's side to help him down with his cart.

"This's as far as I go," he said, pointing to the dirt drive that led away on the other side of the highway.

As the truck pulled off in that direction, a long stream of dust billowing out behind it, Arthur looked slowly about him. On either side the highway sloped down toward the river valley, and he knew it would be no trouble to set his cart rolling down toward the bottoms. Behind him, however, on the side of the road, at the very top of the rise, sat an old abandoned wooden church, its windows boarded up, its signboard blown down, its cross nowhere to be seen.

"Far as I go, too," said Arthur to himself, wheeling slowly over toward its gaping doorway.

# Chapter 18

THE LITTLE church was Arthur's haven for a night, two nights, three nights . . . almost before he knew it, for a week. Inside he had found it dirty but dry. A dozen or so long pews were scattered at odd angles around its small interior, and a tall wooden lectern that Arthur surmised had served for a pulpit lay tipped on its side in a corner. The door hung open on broken hinges, but Arthur found he could wedge it shut quite well with an old board. He pushed a couple of pews together, seat edge to seat edge, and padded them for a bed with some old quilting scraps he found in the basement. He found the pump in the basement too, and by dint of hanging tight to its handle and swinging himself right off the ground several dozen times in a row, he got it flowing again. The water came out sour and rusty at first, but soon fresh clear water came gushing through, and he found he could even pump up enough to get the rusted old toilet working. He found a broom down there, too, and by doing a little bit each day soon managed to sweep the church clean of all the litter that had accumulated there, mostly, he imagined, from small animals. He sat the lectern upright in its corner and rearranged all the pews, aside from the two he used for his bed, around the outside walls. He decided not to open the boarded-up windows, because there was no glass left in them, but he did find a few planks he could slip out easily during the day to let light in.

He also found, almost from the very beginning, a remarkable food supply. On the morning of the second day of his residence, he wheeled himself out through the front door and onto the church's little wooden porch, only one step up from ground level, just in time to watch a heavy, open-backed trailer truck come groaning slowly up the hill from the west. As it finally crossed the top of the rise, its driver shifted gears abruptly, the load jostled about, sending small things flying, and the truck surged forward and on down the other side of the hill, back down toward the river. Arthur lowered his cart down the single step to ground level and scuttled quickly over to the side of the road, where he soon gathered for himself, with no exertion, ten lovely ears of corn. Several of these he immediately boiled up on the wood-burning stove in the little shed attached to the rear of the church, where, no doubt, church suppers had once been prepared. The others he stored away in the basement.

When he had eaten, and done another small spell of cleaning, he scooted around to the front of the church again and found that he did, indeed, live on a bountiful highway. For even as he sat there and watched, truck after truck ground its way slowly up the slope, shifted gears passing the church at the top of the hill, and scattered fragments of its load off to both sides as it went roaring away down the hill in the other direction. In the quiet moments between, when one truck had headed off downhill and another not yet begun its long noisy climb up from the other side, Arthur wheeled himself quickly out to the roadside, gathered as much as he could hold on the cart between his legs or inside his shirt, and scurried back to the church porch, to dump his bounty of corn and potatoes and sugar beets, and head back for another load.

Thus did the early autumn days rush by for Arthur, as, putting from his mind all thoughts of ever again seeing Stella, who had lucklessly been revealed as his sister, when it was by no means as a sister that he had wanted her—indeed, thankful that she was not likely ever to be able to find him here, with his homing device now obviously dead, and that he himself had gone as far as he would, according to the agreement made with himself, and had, now, nowhere more to go—he busied himself with putting the old church back into livable shape, gathering in for storage the harvest that was dropped virtually at his doorstep each day, and wheeling about the top and upper slopes of his little hill, overlooking the Minnesota River, to gather in a supply of firewood.

In his second week of residence he also found, leaning against the side of the building where apparently it had been dumped when the church was abandoned, the signboard on which, with movable letters, the text for the coming Sunday had been announced. The name of the church which had been painted at the top was long since weathered away, the glass facing of the signboard was gone, and quite a few of the letters which had made up its final message were missing, so that what Arthur saw when he laid it on the ground face up read:

I W L   IVE THIS C TY   NTO   HE   AND O   T   E KING     BA  YLO ,
AND HE S  AL  BUR    T W   H FIRE.

ER  M AH  34:2

which Arthur, though no biblical scholar, managed, while waiting patiently over a period of several days for the trucks to leave his usual bounty by the side of the road, to reconstruct, in his mind, for he could not find the missing letters, as follows:

I WILL GIVE THIS CITY INTO THE HAND OF THE KING OF BABYLON, AND HE SHALL BURN IT WITH FIRE.

JEREMIAH  34:2

which Arthur did not think was an especially cheering message, and so soon removed. As the days passed, however, and Arthur's cleaning chores, and the time consumed by them, lessened, and as he waited peacefully in the warm September sun for the next truck to come shuddering by and leave its trail of droppings for him to collect, he began to play with the pile of letters he had plucked from the board, to see what messages he himself might to able to construct from them. The first one he made said:

WHERE ART IS, STELLA ISNT EVER

and though he was pleased with the frankness of it, at first, as he propped it up against the side of the church to see what he had accomplished, by the time he returned to look at it later that same day, he found it depressingly blunt and prosaic. After a great deal of tinkering, he managed by nightfall to come up with:

which he found, when he looked upon it the following morning, at least more poetic and interesting, if still all too painfully true, and so he let it stand for several days. During that time, he also experimented with substituting his name for Stella's, but lacking a second u he had to misspell it ARTHER, which he found displeasingly ugly.

The making of such signs became, as September slipped away, a pleasurable and challenging pastime with which to fill the hours waiting for the harvest-laden trucks to pass his way. He removed the board and letters to the porch, where he sat in relative comfort to puzzle out texts relevant to his situation, and when he made one that he particularly liked, he spaced the letters out nicely on the board and then propped it up against the front of the church, for any passers-by to see, though he honestly doubted that any noticed. His special favorites he let stand for several days. Always, however, he soon became impatient to disassemble them and try out some new combination, if only for his own enlightenment. He tried, for example, questions, such as:

WHAT HAS BEEN RISKED HERE FRIEND

and he tried to achieve his own prophetic tone:

YOU HAVE STOCK IN THIS WORLD
ART 4:32

which was one he especially liked and let remain on the board for several days, and even put back up again, once some time later, for another three-day stand.

With the arrival of October—for Arthur had, in the usual manner of castaways, devised a system for keeping track of the days, which consisted of using an ear of corn to represent each day, without bothering to devise even a single reason for keeping in touch with time—a brief autumn rainy spell drove him indoors. He took his board and letters with him and sat just inside the doorway, where he could still keep his eye on the road. He wanted to be able to scoot out after the fallen produce as soon as possible, lest it get too wet, and be in danger of rotting. But though the inside of the church was dry, and pleasantly clean now, the gray skies had their effect on him, so that he was moved to demand, disconsolately:

LEAVE ARTHUR LIVE ALONE, ALONE

which at least pleased him, for a day or so, with its alliteration, before he was moved to ask, pathetically:

FATHER, WHERE ARE YOU TODAY

and then, having removed that imponderable from the board in a matter of a few hours, to state, cynically:

HERE SITS MELVILLES GREAT IDEA: HA HO 234

With the return of sunshine with the second week of October, however, along with Arthur's growing satisfaction at the amount of food and wood he had already managed to gather in preparation for the coming winter, a considerable portion of the basement now being occupied by great piles of corn, soybeans, sugar beets, squash, potatoes, and kindling, a cheerier and more self-confident mood came over him, so that he was moved from despair to advice, and wrote:

ARTHUR SAYS, EAT A BEET TODAY

He remained inside the doorway now, because though the rains had gone, the chilly nip of true autumn was in the air for all but a few hours in the early afternoon. He preferred not to have to be always carrying the board and letters in and out. And moreover, since the church was on the north side of the road, and its doorway faced south toward the road, and toward that direction into which the sun was declining more and more each day, the best of the sunlight came through the open doorway and fell upon him anyway, so that he was very comfortable. He had only to lean forward to reach through the doorway and lean a newly made text up against the front of the church for all to see. He began to keep the ARTHUR SAYS portion and vary the nature or his advice, until he finally came up with:

ARTHUR SAYS, DONT GO ANYWHERE

which he liked so much that he kept it up for four successive days, an all-time record for his messages.

It was Columbus Day when he decided that that message had been up long enough, and it was time to go to work on a new one. It was a bright, chilly day. The ground had been white with frost when he woke in the morning, he had already brought in several loads of potatoes by mid-morning, and after his last trip out he had also brought in the signboard. He sat in the small square of sunlight, just inside the doorway, to work on it. The board lay in his lap. All the letters had been removed from it, except those which made up ARTHUR SAYS, and spread out neatly on the floor by his side. Working as he always did, devising his message first and then seeing if he had the right letters to complete it, he had just affixed to the board, lightly, for the sake of easy removal in case all the required letters were not there, the first three letters of a new word, so that it read:

ARTHUR SAYS, CON

and was poking around in the pile on the floor to see if he could find the letters to complete his message, when a sudden shadow blocked the doorway and fell across his sign-board.

He looked up, but was unable to tell who it was. The sun was no longer shining outside, but a brilliant glare flooded in through the church door all the same, and around the motionless figure, which was itself encased only in shadow, until at last it stepped farther into the church, and took one step off to the side, and Arthur saw that it was Stella.

"Stella!" he cried. He grabbed the unfinished signboard from his lap and sent it sailing out through the open doorway. It was snowing lightly, as it sometimes does in Minnesota even as early as Columbus Day. Stella dropped to her knees in front of Arthur and threw her arms around him, looks of weariness, joy, pain, beauty, and he knew not what else flashing across her face as she closed in upon his own surprised expression. Then her eyes closed and her mouth pressed down upon his, so that he could not help but respond. It was not the brotherly kiss that he had long since reconciled himself to giving her, should they by unfortunate accident every happen to meet again.

"Oh, Arthur, Arthur," she cried, when at last she stopped for breath. "How I've wanted you! How I've sought you! How I've loved you from the very beginning!" And then she fell to kissing him again, and sent him tumbling to the floor, in the midst of the pile of letters, which went flying in all directions. And though Arthur helplessly, even willingly, joined in at first, bursting with the sudden joy of her reappearance, here, regardless of his knowledge and fears, in his very arms, right now, he felt that he had to break off when he realized, suddenly, that she was fumbling with his clothing, and opened his eyes to see that somehow, without leaving his arms, she had already managed to shed her own skirt and blouse, which lay scattered among the letters on the church floor beside them.

"No, Stella!" he cried, trying to push her away. "We can't do this!"

"Oh, yes we can, Arthur," she laughed, her hands all over him now. "It doesn't make any difference about your legs, we'll manage."

"That's not what I meant," he protested, still unable to keep her busy hands from their work. "You're my sister! I'm your brother! It's true, after all! I found . . ."

"I don't care," she said, shrugging off the last of her own clothes, "I've found you and I love you and I know how you've waited for me and how I want you and I don't care."

"I don't care," she said, one more time, before her mouth came hungrily down on his again.

In the end, Arthur didn't care either.

# PART III

# The End

# Chapter 19

THEY DID very well that first winter, living off what they
playfully termed their "truck garden." As long as the harvest
continued, they went out to the road every morning, and
then again in the afternoon, to gather the produce the trucks
had spilled and carry their own harvest off to storage in the
basement of the church. They laid in a plentiful supply of
firewood as well, and at this Stella was a special help, given
Arthur's limited mobility, especially over rough terrain. And
they made sure that the old church building was closed up as
tight as possible against the rapidly approaching cold weather.
With Arthur's recently acquired mechanical ability and
Stella's dexterity and inventiveness, they managed to devise

a very comfortable shelter, with highly improved arrangements for cooking and heating. They also made love a great deal, and in doing so demonstrated a high level of adaptability to adverse physical circumstances.

When winter came full upon them, and they were left snug and snowbound, Stella and Arthur talked at great length about all that had happened to keep them apart and bring them together. Stella told Arthur some, but not all, of the trials which she had endured in her quest for him. The tracking device, which she had taken from the first as a sign of the true bond between them, had, in an initial flurry of activity, shown Arthur's location as due west; then it had suddenly ceased to function, leaving her in doubt as to whether he was still alive. With Melville in prison, and knowing no more of Arthur's whereabouts then she did, and Kent out of the country, she had only Wells to turn to for help. But Wells, whom she reached first by phone, denied having seen any sign of Arthur, and then, when she visited him in person, at the beginning of July, kept her locked in his office for an entire day and night, scurrying about making obscene propositions to her and accusing her and Arthur of plotting against him. With no one to support or aid her, and not willing to believe, after Wells' frantic behavior, that Arthur was not still alive, she had no choice, she felt, but to take to the road in search of him: as, she suspected, he himself, equally lost and alone, might already have done, returning to his old ways. It was not easy, however. But when Arthur pressed her for details, she declined, saying that it was not important, and that what mattered was where they were now, and that here they were, where they were.

The first indication that her search for Arthur might not be altogether hopeless had come on the outskirts of Paducah,

Kentucky, when she saw, on the opposite side of the road, an elderly man who was also hitchhiking, though in the other direction. He had one thumb out in the air, a golf bag slung over his back, and a strange-looking piece of paper clutched in his other hand. When she crossed the street to examine it more closely, she found it was a certificate for one share of stock in the Poughkeepsie Institute. When she asked the old man, who seemed to her unusually well dressed for a hitchhiker, where he had got it, he said he had blown his big chance with a double bogie on the seventeenth after being two up on the first thirty-six and then his car wouldn't start either, but it didn't matter because he wasn't much going anywhere anyway and could do it just as easily with his thumb as with his car, there were plenty of golf courses.

While all that was of little help to Stella, and the old man was willing to advise her further only on the matter of how to improve her putting stance, she did remember that Melville had once spoken of plans for distributing stock in the Institute, that the matter had been put into Wells' hands, and that, during her imprisonment in his office, Wells had grabbed a manila envelope out of his desk and disappeared briefly, saying that he was going to dispose of the last evidence that might connect him with the entire project, locking her tightly in as he left and returning with a much relieved smile on his face, and a promise to release her in the morning.

Firmly convinced, by all this, that Arthur was not only still alive but was apparently traveling about, probably in search of her, she set about her task of tracking him with renewed vigor. She sought, now, not just Arthur, but visible evidence of his recent presence, in the form of Poughkeepsie Institute stock certificates, and these were not long in appearing, especially in a broad belt lying across the very middle of the country, stretching west, she found, from Ohio into the plains states. There she discovered the certificates in the hands of children, youths, adults, the aged; often among people camped by the roadside or looking for a small home, in a town they "just happened" to be in, where they thought they "might settle down"; frequently in the hands of hitchhikers who claimed that they had gotten rid of their own cars and were now off to "just look around"; and on a few occasions in the hands of motorists who offered to take her anywhere she wanted to go, and were apparently, unlike many others she had met, benevolent in their intentions. Most of these shareholders whom she encountered seemed to remember little, if anything, of from whom, or under what circumstances, they had received their certificates; they only knew that they were gifts, that they were worthless, and that their shares were properly registered. Some even offered to give their certificates to Stella, if it would help her to have something not to worry about, something that was not going anywhere where she would have to track it down. From the many fragments of their recall, she pieced together a picture of what she took to be Arthur, still heading west. She kept on after him.

Her big break came at a rest stop on an interstate freeway in Wisconsin, where she found a large group of people gathered in a tightly packed crowd around the picnic area. Some, on the outer fringes, were holding children on their shoulders, or climbing on top of parked cars. Charmed by the music she heard emerging from the crowd, she gradually made her way in among them until she arrived at the inner edges, where she found, happily ensconced on the grass between a pair of picnic tables, a five-man jazz band, playing "Topsy." In bold, bright letters on the big bass drum, she read "The Poughkeepsie Institute Five." When they stopped for a break, she went over and asked them where they were from.

"We ain't *from* anywhere, baby," said the sax player, "We're *here!*"

When she asked them more specifically about their name, they all pulled out stock certificates, told her how they had been given them only a few days before and had been moved by the idea behind them to set up right where they were for as long a stand as possible. They were well fed and sheltered by tourists, if the highway patrol kicked them out they would just move along to the next rest stop, and in the meantime they were happily working up some new numbers of their own. Would Stella like to hear "Goin' Nowhere"?

She wouldn't, but when she had gotten them to tell her how recently they had seen Arthur and in what direction he was last headed, she left to the sound of its curious melody anyway. They were right, he was only a few days to the west. It took her a few more to locate him exactly, though she had much help. Minnesotans with Poughkeepsie Institute stock certificates seemed to almost line the highways. She could hardly believe that Arthur had had such an enormous supply to pass out. Truth to tell, some explained, he probably didn't. It was rumored that a flourishing counterfeit market had been in operation for several weeks already, but no one seemed bothered by this. A share was a share, an old woman in Red Wing explained to Stella, it was what it was, and if it wasn't worth anything to begin with, what difference did it make whether or not it was counterfeit? Why, Stella asked, would anybody bother to counterfeit them then? Oh, explained the old lady, because so many people wanted them, so many people: they were wanted as gifts for newborns, they were wanted for tokens to place in the caskets of the dead, and there wasn't a soul, it seemed, who just didn't want one to have along with him, just because it was what it was, didn't Stella understand that? Stella wasn't sure, at first, that she did. Then she was given the final lift of her long journey, driven almost to Arthur's very doorstep, by the fourth-place Beavers of the Three-I League, Class D, who had abandoned their schedule with eleven games left to play in order to visit the Black Hills, but had instead ended up spending three weeks in the Wisconsin Dells and were only now on the way to their original goal. They told Stella of rumors that an attempt to trade Poughkeepsie Institute shares on the New York Stock Exchange had failed because, although everybody wanted one, nobody wanted more than one. They told her that an active underworld ring dealing in stolen certificates had dissolved in dismay within weeks when they were unable to find, for these items which supposedly everyone in the country wanted, a single buyer. They told her that U.S. Government attempts to suppress all the activity in Poughkeepsie Institute stock by flooding the market with phony certificates had not only failed to devalue them but had provided a much-needed additional supply to share with friends abroad. They told her that there wasn't anyone who had one who wouldn't willingly give it away, without for a moment feeling that he was being deprived of something. They told her that they each had one, given to them by Arthur himself, and asked her if she had one. She said no, she must be the only person in the country by now who didn't have one.

"No," said Arthur, snuggling up against her in the little bed he had made out of two church pews, while a Minnesota blizzard raged outside, "I don't have one either."

"With or without them," said Stella, "here we are."

"Tell me," said Arthur, "what did it sound like, that song they were playing?"

" 'Goin' Nowhere'?" said Stella. "I don't really know, it was a very curious melody, there was no way of telling what note to expect next."

PSYCHOLOGICAL SERVICES DEPT.

PS
3557
R377
G6

Greenberg, Alvin.
    Going nowhere.

PS3557 R377 G6
+Going nowhere; a+Greenberg, Alvin

0 00 02 0208960 3
MIDDLEBURY COLLEGE

DEMCO